Praise for the Alcatraz Series

"This is an excellent choice to read aloud to the whole family. It's funny, exciting, and briskly paced."
—NPR on *Alcatraz vs. the Evil Librarians*

"Genuinely funny . . . Plenty here to enjoy."
—*Locus* on *Alcatraz vs. the Evil Librarians*

"Like Lemony Snicket and superhero comics rolled into one (and then revved up on steroids), this nutty novel . . . [is] also sure to win passionate fans."
—*Publishers Weekly* (starred review) on *Alcatraz vs. the Evil Librarians*

"The conventional trappings of the middle-school fantasy get turned upside down in this zany novel. . . . Readers who prefer fantasy with plenty of humor should enjoy entering Alcatraz's strange but amusing world."   —*School Library Journal* on *Alcatraz vs. the Evil Librarians*

"In this original, hysterical homage to fantasy literature, Sanderson's first novel for youth recalls the best in Artemis Fowl and A Series of Unfortunate Events. The humor, although broad enough to engage preteens, is also sneakily aimed at adults. . . . And as soon as they finish the last wickedly clever page, they will be standing in line for more from this seasoned author."   —*VOYA* on *Alcatraz vs. the Evil Librarians*

"A thoroughly thrilling read."

> —*The Horn Book* on *The Scrivener's Bones*

"Those who enjoy their fantasy with a healthy dose of slapstick humor will be delighted. Give this novel to fans of Eoin Colfer's Artemis Fowl and Catherine Jinks's Cadel Piggott in *Evil Genius*. They will appreciate Sanderson's cheerful sarcastic wit and none-too-subtle digs at librarians."

> —*School Library Journal* on *The Scrivener's Bones*

"Every bit as clever, fast-paced, and original as [the first book] . . . Howlingly funny for adults, older teens who can be persuaded to read a 'juvenile' novel, and exceptionally bright middle schoolers."

> —*VOYA* on *The Scrivener's Bones*

"With comical insight into human nature and just enough substance to make it all matter, the plot offers up plenty of action, gadgetry, metafictional humor, grudgingly dispensed hints of the Librarians' endgame, and counterintuitive Smedry Talents to keep the old fans and new readers alike turning pages."

> —*The Horn Book* on *The Knights of Crystallia*

"Offbeat humor, a budding romance, plenty of magic, creative world-building, smart references to science fiction luminaries, clever wordplay, and good action scenes make this one a strong choice for young teen boys and adult fans of the SF genre. . . . Hard to imagine it being any better written."

> —*VOYA* on *The Knights of Crystallia*

"Lives up to its predecessors with vivid action and high drama."
—*Midwest Book Review* on *The Knights of Crystallia*

"Beneath the wild humor, there are surprisingly subtle messages about responsibility and courage."
—*School Library Journal* on *The Knights of Crystallia*

"As goofy randomness streamlines into compelling narration, even readers who don't find giant robots reason alone to pick up a book will be drawn into Alcatraz's cohesive world, with its unique form of magic."
—*The Horn Book* on *The Shattered Lens*

"I love this series! Sanderson's one of the few writers of adult fiction I've read who can also write effortlessly and dead-on true for kids as well. This is a fabulous book to read aloud! It's not only funny and has plenty of action, but the series has got heart as well. Highly recommended!"
—*YA Books Central* on *The Shattered Lens*

BY BRANDON SANDERSON

ALCATRAZ VS. THE EVIL LIBRARIANS

Alcatraz vs. the Evil Librarians
The Scrivener's Bones
The Knights of Crystallia
The Shattered Lens
The Dark Talent

The Rithmatist

THE MISTBORN TRILOGY

Mistborn
The Well of Ascension
The Hero of Ages

THE RECKONERS

Steelheart
Firefight
Calamity

ALCATRAZ VS. THE EVIL LIBRARIANS

THE DARK TALENT

BRANDON SANDERSON

Illustrations by
HAYLEY LAZO

STARSCAPE

A Tom Doherty Associates Book ∗ New York

THE DARK TALENT

Copyright © 2016 by Dragonsteel Entertainment, LLC

Illustrations copyright © 2016 by Dragonsteel Entertainment, LLC

Reading and Activity Guide copyright © 2016 by Tor Books

Brandon Sanderson® is a registered trademark of Dragonsteel Entertainment, LLC

Illustrations by Hayley Lazo
Map by Isaac Stewart

A Starscape Book
Published by Tom Doherty Associates, LLC
175 Fifth Avenue
New York, NY 10010

www.tor-forge.com

The Library of Congress Cataloging-in-Publication Data
is available upon request.

ISBN 978-0-7653-8140-8 (hardcover)
ISBN 978-1-4668-8153-2 (e-book)

Our books may be purchased in bulk for promotional, educational, or business use. Please contact your local bookseller or the Macmillan Corporate and Premium Sales Department at 1-800-221-7945, extension 5442, or by e-mail at MacmillanSpecialMarkets@macmillan.com.

First Edition: September 2016

Printed in the United States of America

0 9 8 7 6 5 4 3 2 1

For Barb Sanderson
Who knows the real Alcatraz

Author's Foreword

I am a coward.

Oh, did you expect more of a foreword than that? You expected me to be witty, entertaining, or at the very least informative? Well . . . being a coward, I suppose I will cave in to your expectations.

This is normally the part of the story where I make fun of you for forgetting what has happened so far. But I'm too afraid of how you'll react to be properly condescending. Instead, accept this quick recap:

1. I am a Smedry, and my ancestors trapped a dark power inside our bloodline, preventing it from destroying the world. It manifests as Talents granted to all Smedrys, and though each Talent looks like a huge liability at first, they can be employed in cool ways. At least, that's how things *used* to work. Unfortunately, I released this power—known as the Dark Talent, which somehow relates to my Talent for breaking things. Releasing that broke my family's powers, dooming the world. Oops.

2. My father, Attica Smedry, is slavishly dedicated to giving every person on earth a Smedry Talent, which the rest of us think would cause mass chaos. I let my father out of his prison, gave him the tools he needed to pursue his crazy quest, and undoubtedly doomed the world. Oops.

3. The Librarians are a force bent on controlling information and keeping everyone in the Hushlands (Librarian-controlled areas like Europe, Asia, and the Americas) from learning about awesome things like magic and cheese puffs that don't stain your fingers orange. They attacked the Free Kingdom of Mokia, and during that conflict I ended up as king. (Don't ask.) As part of my reckless plan to drive the Librarians away, my friend (and sworn knight-protector) Bastille got shot and is now in a coma. The only way to save her is to infiltrate the Highbrary, a center of Librarian power inside the Hushlands—and the only way to do *that* is to rely upon my mother, Shasta Smedry, an evil Librarian to the core. She's undoubtedly going to betray us somehow, then find a way to (yes) doom the world. Oops.

4. I've now figured out how to use footnotes.*

The sad thing is, it just gets worse from here. Some of you have been waiting for years to read this, the final volume of my autobiography. You've written to me, asking if the Librarians have somehow suppressed its publication.

---

* Obviously, the world is doomed as a result. Oops.

I wish that were true. I wish I could tell you some external force had prevented me from finishing this story.

That's not what happened.

This last volume took so long because I am a coward. I really, really didn't want to write it. The finale of this story covers the most painful part of my young life, including my biggest failures—both to my family and to the world at large.

This is where the story stops being funny.

You've been warned.

ALCATRAZ
· VS. THE ·
EVIL LIBRARIANS

THE
DARK
TALENT

Chapter

Doug

So there I was, standing in my chambers on the day before the world ended, facing my greatest adversary to date.

The royal wardrobe coordinator.

Janie was a perky Nalhallan woman wearing trendy Free Kingdomer clothing. Technically you could describe her outfit as a tunic—but it was only similar to a tunic in the same way that a high-end sports car is similar to a broken-down pickup. It was more like a dress with a belt at the waist, and had a large bow on one side with stylish embroidery up the sleeves.

It looked nice, making it a complete contrast to the monstrosity she held up for me to wear.

"That," I said, "is a *clown costume*."

"What?" Janie said. "Of course it isn't."

"It's a white jumpsuit," I said, "with fluffy pink bobs over the buttons!"

"White for the purity of the throne, Your Former Highness," Janie said, "and pink to indicate your magnanimous decision to step down peacefully."

"It has oversized floppy shoes."

"A representation of your magnificent footprint upon the kingdom, Your Former Highness."

"And the fake flower to squirt water?"

"So that you may shower all who approach you with symbolic waters of life."

I raised a skeptical eyebrow at her and walked over to the bed, picking up the poofy rainbow clown wig she'd brought for me to wear.

"Obviously," Janie said, "that is a representation of the varieties of cultures and peoples you served during your kingship." She smiled.

"Let me guess," I said, tossing the wig onto the bed. "The Librarians took this 'regal' costume worn by retired Mokian kings and, where I'm from, gave it to clowns. That turned it into something ridiculous in the Hushlands, like how they named prisons after famous Free Kingdomers."

"Uh, yeah," Janie said. "Sure . . . Uh, that's . . . exactly what happened."

I frowned at her evasiveness. At the moment, I wore only a bathrobe. My old clothing—green jacket, T-shirt, jeans—was gone. My jacket had been cut up, and the rest of my clothing had been vaporized in a rather unfortunate incident containing far too much Alcatraz nudity.

Outside my room, Tuki Tuki—capital city of Mokia—was utterly silent. The drums of celebration had stopped, as had the songs of joy. Their day of celebration past, the Mokians now mourned in silence to highlight the voices among them that had been quieted.

If I was right, that silence was about to get a *lot* worse. I refer you to the footnote* for proof.

"What else do you have?" I asked Janie.

"Well, let's see," she said, obviously disappointed I wouldn't wear the clown outfit. I might be a former king of Mokia—though I'd only served for one day—but if that was the traditional costume of my station, I'd go without.

She reached into her large trunk and pulled out what appeared to be a dog costume, with furred feet, a tail, and a headpiece with floppy ears.

"No," I said immediately.

"But it's the official outfit for a retired prince of—"

---

* People who use footnotes in books are very smart, and you can trust what they say.

"No."

Janie sighed, setting it on the bed and digging farther into her trunk.

"What is it with these 'traditional' outfits?" I said, poking the dog costume. "I mean, even without Librarian interference, you have to admit they're kind of . . ."

"Regal?"

"Ridiculous," I said. "It's almost like you *want* your former kings to look silly."

Janie shifted. "Uh . . . why would we want to do that? It's not like we want people to see former monarchs as foolish, so a ruler who has stepped down can never change his mind, stage a coup, and seize back the kingdom." She forced out a laugh.

"You're a terrible liar."

"Thank you! How about this nice cat costume? It represents the way you gracefully maneuvered the politics of the throne!"

"No animal costumes at all, please."

She sighed, then continued digging in her trunk. A moment later she cursed under her breath. The lights at the sides of the trunk had stopped working.

Curious, I walked over. Why did she even *need* lights? I soon saw that the inside of the trunk was much larger than the outside would indicate. The trunk was a neat trick, but nothing I hadn't seen before—in the Free Kingdoms, people use different varieties of glass to accomplish some pretty amazing things.*

The lights at the sides were made of a special kind of glass to provide illumination—and that glass was powered by a special type of sand called brightsand. It worked somewhat like a battery for glass. (In the same way that shipwrecked people act like batteries for sharks.†)

Her brightsand for the lights appeared to have lost its charge. Fortunately, I knew something else that worked as a battery for both sand *and* sharks: me.

I reached out and touched the glass of her lights. I might have—somehow—broken the Smedry Talents, but I was still an Oculator. That meant I could power special types of glass.

I dredged up something inside me and pushed it out— it was a little like trying to throw up when not nauseous. The glass lights shining into Janie's trunk burst aglow, brilliant as the sun. I yelped, startled by the sudden explosion of power. Usually there was a sense of resistance when trying to do this, but today the energy came right out.

I stumbled back as the glass plates actually *melted*.

---

* Like adding footnotes to books.
† It's true. Think about it.

"Wow," Janie said. "Uh . . . you *really* hate these clothes, don't you?"

"I . . ."

Let me pause here and explain an important point. When you are a coward like me, you should always take credit for something you didn't intend to do. You see, part of being a coward is being too afraid of not being seen as awesome to admit to not being awesome, though you have to be careful not to let on that you're too afraid of not being awesome to admit that not being awesome would indicate to those that want someone to be awesome that you are not as awesome as your awesomeness would otherwise indicate.

"I'm awesome," I said.

Sorry. I got a little confused in that last paragraph. Man, this writing can be as regal as a former Mokian monarch sometimes.

Janie looked at me.

"Ah, ahem," I said. "I saw a military uniform. What about that?"

I'd only seen a glimpse of it in the bright light: an outfit of Nalhallan design, with big epaulettes* on the shoulders

---

* Epaulettes are those things soldiers wear on their shoulders to make them look more important. Nothing proclaims "Look how macho I am"

and all kinds of ropes and ribbons and buttons and things, intended to make officers stand out on a battlefield and get shot first so the soldiers doing the real fighting are safe.

"I suppose," Janie said, "I can try to dig that out—but I'll need to install some new lights first." She glanced at the bubbling globs of glass on the sides of her trunk.

"Uh, thanks," I said.

"You *sure* you don't want a frog costume? Technically it's supposed to be for a retired king who served at least seven days, but you could swing it."

"No thanks." I hesitated, but was too curious not to ask. "Let me guess. The frog costume represents how a monarch leaps hurdle after hurdle as a leader?"

"Nah. It's symbolic of how you survived your kingship without croaking."

Of course.

Janie got out another pack and began digging around for some lights. Embarrassed at having ruined her glass, I made an excuse about needing to use the restroom and slipped out. In truth, I just wanted to be alone for a little while.

---

more than a good set of epaulettes. Other than, I guess, a big sign that reads LOOK HOW MACHO I AM, but we wouldn't want to be *flagrant* about it, would we?

The hallway outside my room was decorated with a woven mat, the walls constructed of large reeds, the roof thatched. I didn't see a soul. The place was freakishly quiet, and I found myself tiptoeing. (A common action of cowards like me.)

It seemed to me that with everything that had happened in the last few days, I should be doing something far more important than deciding what to wear. Tuki Tuki was safe, but I hadn't won this war. Not as long as Bastille and so many Mokians lay in comas, Librarians still ruled the Hushlands, and there were footnotes lying scattered around unused.*

We needed to chase down my father and stop him from putting his insane plan into motion. Though . . . maybe his plan wouldn't work anymore. I'd broken the Talents, after all. Maybe that would stop him from giving Talents to everyone else.

No, I thought. *This is my father.* He'd bested the undead Librarians of Alexandria and had uncovered the secret of the Sands of Rashid. He would be able to do this too. If we didn't stop him.

I heard voices in the hallway, so I followed them to a

---

* There. That's better.

spacious room topped by lazy ceiling fans. Inside, my grandfather stood before a large wall of glowing glass that showed the faces of numerous people in a variety of ethnic costumes. I recognized them as the monarchs of the Free Kingdoms—I'd saved their lives at one point. Maybe two. I lose count.

Bald on top, my grandfather wore a bushy mustache and had an equally bushy ring of white hair that puffed out along the back of his head, like he'd been in an epic pillow fight and a mass of stuffing had gotten stuck to his scalp. He was, as always, decked out in a stylish tuxedo.

"Now, I don't want to act ungrateful," my grandfather was saying to the monarchs, "but . . . Accountable Abercrombies, people! Don't you think you're a little late?"

"Mokia asked for aid," said Queen Kamiko, an Asian-looking woman in her fifties.

"Yes," agreed a man wearing a European-looking crown. I didn't know his name. "You wanted armies. We're sending them, along with the air guard, to help you Smedrys. What is the complaint?"

"My complaint?" Grandpa Smedry sputtered. "The war is over! My grandson won it!"

"Yes, well," said a dark-skinned monarch in a colorful hat. "Certainly there is still work to be done. Cleanup, reconstruction, that sort of thing."

"You cowards," I said, stepping into the room.

Trust me. I know how to spot cowards.

My grandfather looked toward me, as did the monarchs on the screen. The Free Kingdomers claim that they are nothing like the Hushlanders, but things like this glass wall—which was Communicator's Glass, designed for speaking over long distances—are very similar to Hushlander technology. The two could be sides to the same coin.

Ditto for those monarchs and the leaders of the Librarians. Politicians, it seemed, often shared more with one another than they did with the people they represented.

"Lad . . ." Grandpa Smedry said.

"I will speak to them," I said, stepping up beside him.

"But—" Grandpa said.

"I won't be shushed!"

"I wasn't going to shush you," Grandpa said. "I was going to point out that you're addressing the world's collected monarchs in a *bathrobe*."

Uh . . .

Right.

"It's a representation of my disdain for their callous disregard for Mokian lives!" I proclaimed, raising a hand with my finger pointed toward the sky.

Thanks, Janie.

"Young Smedry," said Kamiko, "we are grateful for what you have done, but you have no right to speak to us in such a way!"

"I have *every* right!" I snapped. "I am a former king of Mokia."

"You were king for *one day*," said a tiny dinosaur. I knew that one: Supremus Rex, monarch of the dinosaurs.

"One day is long enough to get some of the stench on me," I said, "but brief enough to not be overwhelmed by it. You send armies *now*? After the fight is won, and you realize that an alliance with the Librarians is impossible? I can't believe that you—"

"I don't have to listen to this," Kamiko interrupted, turning off her section of the glass. The others followed suit, switching off their screens until only one remained, a man with red hair and beard, looking sorrowful. Brig, the High King, Bastille's father.

I felt my anger fade, and I looked sheepishly at my grandfather. I'd stormed in and ruined his meeting.

"That was quite energetic!" Grandpa Smedry said. "I approve."

"I don't know," another voice said from the back of the room. My uncle Kaz was there, sitting and sipping a fruit drink, his adventuring hat on the table beside him.

Four feet tall—and please don't call him a dwarf or a midget—Kaz was dressed in a leather jacket and sturdy hiking boots. He had a pair of Warrior's Lenses hanging from his pocket; he wasn't an Oculator, but he was pretty handy in a fight.

Kaz raised his cup toward me. "It was good calling them cowards, Al, but I think you could have slipped another insult or two in before they switched off their glass. And the send-off . . . yeah, that wasn't suitably theatrical at all."

"True, true," Grandpa said. "The dramatic effect of your intrusion *could* have been much greater, and you could have been far more annoying."

And that's probably the best introduction I could give you to my family. In the last six months of my life, I'd taunted undead Librarian ghosts, recklessly used my Talent to lay waste to armies, run headlong into danger a dozen times over, and aggravated some of the most powerful Librarians who have ever lived—but compared to the rest of the Smedry clan, I'm the *responsible, cool-headed* one.

"I doubt insulting the monarchs will do any good, Leavenworth," the High King said to my grandfather, speaking through his glowing pane of glass. "They *are* afraid. A few days ago the world made sense to them—but now everything has changed."

"Because the Librarians were driven off?" I asked. Bastille's father looked very, very tired, with red eyes and drooping features.

"Yes," the king said to me. "Driven off by one person, and by a power they didn't know he had—a power they can't imagine or understand. They're afraid that what you have done will enrage the Librarians."

"Mokia was their sacrifice," Grandpa Smedry said, angry. "They foolishly hoped it would satiate the Librarians. And now they're convinced that the Librarians will return in force, determined this time to crush the entirety of the Free Kingdoms."

Politics.

I *hate* politics. When I'd first learned about the Free Kingdoms, I'd imagined how wonderful and amazing they'd be. I spent two entire books trying to get there, only to find that—despite their many wonders—the people in them were . . . well, people.* Free Kingdomers had all the flaws of people in the Hushlands, except with sillier clothing.

I thought of Bastille, unconscious. She'd be so embarrassed to be seen that way. Those monarchs had abandoned her, and Mokia, for their own petty games. It made

---

* I guess I was expecting marmosets?

me angry. Angry at the monarchs, angry at the Librarians, angry at the *world*. I sneered, stepping forward, and
slapped my hands against the Communicator's Glass on
the wall.

"Lad?" Grandpa Smedry asked.

The glass beneath my fingers began to glow.

Perhaps I should have been wary, considering what
I'd done to Janie's lights. I just wanted to *do* something. I
powered the wall glass. I threw everything I had into those
panels, causing them to shine brightly.

"You can't call them back," Kaz said, "not unless they
allow you to—"

I pushed *something* into that glass, something powerful. I had certain advantages, being raised in the Hushlands. Everyone in the Free Kingdoms had expectations
about what was and wasn't possible.

I was too stupid to know what they knew, and I was too
much a Smedry to let that bother me.

What I did next defies explanation. But since it's my
job to convey difficult concepts to you, I'm going to try
anyway. Imagine jumping off a high building into a sea
of marshmallows, then reaching out with a million arms
to touch the entire world, while realizing that every emotion you've ever had is connected to every other emotion,
and they're really one big emotion, like an emotion-whale

that you can't completely see because you're up too close to notice anything other than a little bit of leathery emotion-whale skin.

I let out a deep breath.

Wow.

In that moment, the squares of Communicator's Glass each winked back on. They showed the rooms of the monarchs, most of whom were still there, though they'd stood from their chairs to speak with their attendants. One had gotten a sandwich. Another was playing solitaire.*

They looked at me, and I somehow knew that my face had appeared on each of their panes of glass, large and dominating.

"I," I told them, "am going to the Highbrary."

Is that my voice?

"You are worried I've started something dangerous," I said. "You're wrong. I'm not starting it, I'm *finishing* it. The Librarians have terrorized us for far too long. I intend to make certain *they* are the ones who are frightened and *they* are the ones, for once, who have to worry about what they're going to lose.

---

* Yes, solitaire. What, you think kings and queens are always doing important stuff, like chopping off heads and invading neighboring kingdoms?

"Some of you are scared. Some of you are selfish. The rest of you are downright ignorant. Well, you're going to have to put those things aside, because you can't ignore what's coming. I know something the Librarians don't. The end is here. You can't stop this war from progressing. So it's time for you to stand up, stop whining, and either help or *get out of my way.*"

I let go of the glass. The images winked off, the wall turning dark.

"Now *that*," Kaz said from behind, "is how you end a conversation with style!"

Chapter

Lilly

Once upon a time there was a boy.

This should come as no surprise, as approximately half the world's population is—or at one time was—boys.

This boy got into trouble a lot, as should also be no surprise. Everyone gets into a lot of trouble when they are young—well, everyone but that kid Reginald down the street, but nobody likes him anyway.

Something was different about this boy. Often when he got into trouble, it wasn't his fault. Like, actually not his fault—rather than "My little brother did it" or "I swear I have no idea why that empty cookie bag is under my bed" or "I really didn't mean to invade Poland." No, this kid truly did nothing wrong.

Things just broke around him.

Well, a lifetime of being blamed for things he didn't do beat this kid down pretty hard. He had basically given up on life, until one day something changed. *He became part of a family. He discovered he was famous. He was told that he was special.*

From there, an amazing trend began. He started to succeed. Things started to go right for him. This trend should have worried him, because if he'd learned one lesson in life, it was that when things broke around him, they broke really, really badly.

He started to live as if he could do anything, no matter how bold, no matter how outrageous. He went on one last adventure, he struggled and had some tough times, but then everything turned out fine in the end. So that's nice.

The above is what we call a fairy tale, and it's a modern one, not one from the past. How do we know the difference?

Because in this one, the ending is a lie.

"So . . ." Kaz said from the back of the room. "Infiltrating the Highbrary, eh? The Library of Congress?"

"Uh, yeah," I replied.

---

* Well, to be more precise, *all things changed.*

"And telling everyone about it," Kaz continued, "including the Librarian sympathizers on the Council of Kings—who are sure to tell their allies we're coming."

"Er, exactly."

"Bold," Kaz said. "Almost stupid."

"The Smedry way?" I said.

Kaz stood up, pulling on his hat. "Close enough."

"Think of it like this, Son," Grandpa said to Kaz. "Attica is on his way to the Highbrary too. What young Alcatraz has done is make it far more difficult for his father to get in, giving us more time."

"Besides," I said, trying to sort through why I'd said what I had, "if there's an antidote for the coma that Bastille and the Mokians are in, we should be able to find it at the Highbrary."

"Sounds almost rational when you two put it that way," Kaz said. "Well, don't worry. It shouldn't matter if the Librarians know we're coming, as I can simply use my Talent to sneak us into . . ." He trailed off. For a moment, he'd obviously forgotten that I'd broken the Talents. His face fell. "Right. Slipped my mind. So how *are* we going to get in?"

"Well," Grandpa said, "first we engage in a complex campaign of political misdirection. I'll put forward a motion in the Nalhallan chamber of politics, for discussion by the Council of Kings, with the goal of invoking extended sanctions against Librarian sympathizers."

"Oh, economic sanctions!" Kaz said. "Fun stuff!"

"Then we will institute a lengthy but determined campaign of political propaganda inside the Hushlands, brewing discontent among the general populace so that we can eventually recruit some of the guards who watch the defenses around Washington, DC."

"Wow, political propaganda! Just the kind of exciting stuff people want from an action-adventure story."

"Precisely," Grandpa said. "Then, after years of toil and effort, we will convince one of the Hushlander malcontents to post a note on the head Librarian's door, condemning him and creating an international incident. In the chaos that follows, we can get ourselves assigned as ambassadors and move into the city, thereby completing step one of a seventeen-step process of getting into the place unseen!"

"Fantastic!" Kaz said.

We all stood around for a moment looking at each other. The silence in the city was pervasive, at least until something very loud detonated nearby, throwing debris against the outside walls and shaking us all with the blast.

"Huh," Grandpa said. "I guess, alternatively, we could

run away from the unexplained explosion, steal a ship, and fly into the Hushlands with guns blazing."

"Oh, thank *goodness*," I said. "I'm going to be writing my autobiography someday, and all that stuff you described sounds like it would be *really* boring to write."

We scrambled out of the room and into the hallway beyond, which was suddenly bustling with activity. The explosion, it seemed, had shocked the life into people.* We pushed through the rushing Mokians before being confronted by a ring of guards with face paint and spears. In their center stood Queen Kamali, a tall Mokian woman in her late teens.

"We didn't do it!" Kaz said immediately.

"I didn't assume you had, Lord Kazan," the queen replied. "This is a Librarian missile strike. We suffered them periodically during the years before the actual invasion." She eyed me. "Of course, there's a chance that something provoked them into sending this particular attack."

"Uh . . ." I said. "How do you know . . . ?"

"About your ultimatum? It was displayed on every piece of glass in the palace, Lord Alcatraz."

---

* Those it hadn't shocked the life *out* of.

It *was?* Seems I went a little overboard with powering that Communicator's Glass.

"In the past," the queen said, "these attacks were merely an annoyance, for we had our protective dome. Without it, the attack could be devastating. I'm ordering everyone into the shelters." She hesitated. "I don't suppose you'll come?"

"Are there snacks?" Kaz asked.

Another explosion shook the city. Aluki, of the royal guard, grabbed the queen by the shoulder. "We must go. Leave the Smedrys to do what they do best."

"Save the world?" Grandpa asked.

"Get into trouble?" Kaz asked.

"Run around screaming?" I asked.

"Draw fire," Aluki said, towing the queen away, her guards going with them.

Grandpa grinned, then led the way, finger thrust forward as he ran down the hallway. We joined him, Kaz moving the most quickly since he'd put on his Warrior's Lenses. My own Lenses were in Grandpa's care for the moment. Since I'd been resting from my ordeal the day before, he'd taken them to be polished and inspected for chips.

We charged down one corridor, then another, and eventually spurted out a large doorway and onto a field

full of enormous glass animals. Vehicles, after the Free
Kingdomer style. A sly raven, a proud griffin, a majestic
eagle, and . . . a penguin.

"You're going to pick the penguin, aren't you?" I said
with a sigh as Grandpa started running across the field.

"Of course, lad! It's the most elegant of the choices."

Right. Well, I'd been looking forward to flying to the
Hushlands, but sailing would probably work too.

Rockets fell from the sky over the collection of retro
huts and wooden structures that made up Tuki Tuki. Each
rocket trailed a plume of smoke as it roared down past the
broken remnants of the city's protective dome. A nearby
explosion shook the ground and I stumbled, angry. First
the siege, now this. The Librarians couldn't even let the
people of Tuki Tuki mourn their fallen friends and family.
Instead they launched an air strike the day after the siege
broke—evidently with the attitude of, "If we can't have it,
we'll just blow it up."

"Wait, Grandpa!" I yelled. "My mother! We've got to
take her."

"I'm not convinced of that!" Grandpa yelled back.

"We're bringing her," I said. Yes, she was a Librarian.
Yes, Grandpa was right not to trust her. But my mother
was the one who had guessed where my father would go
next; she knew him better than even Grandpa did.

My Truthfinder's Lens had confirmed she wasn't lying about my father. She'd been working to stop Attica for years now. My instincts said we'd need her before this infiltration was finished. As a side note,* my life involves some of the strangest lines of dialogue you'll ever read. Case in point:

"Fine," Grandpa said. "You fetch your evil Librarian mother from the jail. I'll go warm up the giant penguin!"

"I'll join you, Al," Kaz said as I bolted through the town toward the jail—or, well, the improvised jail that we'd set up for my mother.

Tuki Tuki had once been an idyllic place of flowers, green grass, and smiling faces. Now it was mostly broken-up ground, pieces of fallen glass, and trampled flowers. The missiles added smoldering craters for variety's sake.

The evacuation into the shelters seemed to be going well though, as large masses of people were disappearing safely into underground bunkers. Before too long, we were running through an almost empty city. Well, empty save for death missiles dropping down upon us. I was pleased to find that I'd been through so many crazy situations like this that I almost wasn't panicked by that idea.

---

* Which is completely different from a footnote.

"So," Kaz said, keeping pace with me easily because of his sunglasses, "any idea when you'll be able to . . . you know . . . bring the Talents back?"

I shook my head.

"You sure?"

"I—"

I cut off as a missile dropped in our direction. We dove for shelter beside a wall as the missile hit right beyond us, then *bounced* before coming to a stop. We waited, tense, but no explosion followed.

"A dud," Kaz said. "Let's go."

I followed, passing uncomfortably close to the missile. Something odd about it struck me. "The entire back half is made of glass," I said. "So much for the Librarians avoiding the use of Free Kingdomer technology."*

"A lot of them do avoid it," Kaz said. "But then again, a lot of them think that only *they* should be able to use stuff like this. Remember, being a Librarian of Biblioden is all about control. They don't want unworthies to have access to things like glass. Those missiles fly farther and lighter using brightsand to power their engines—but the explosives are probably all Hushlander

---

* Which all seems to involve glass for some reason or another. Don't ask me. I think it's weird too.

TNT or some such, which is a lot cheaper than the silimatic equivalent."

"Hypocrites."

"Yeah. The only things the Librarians *haven't* ever been able to steal from us are the Talents." He hesitated, and then obviously couldn't help pushing a little further. "So, what exactly *did* you do, anyway? Maybe we can figure out how to bring them back by looking at the way you broke them."

I grimaced. "I don't know *what* I did, Kaz. It was like . . . I grew tired of trying to control the Talent, and I let it go. Let it do what it wanted."

"You make it sound alive," Kaz said, turning down another desolate street.

"It kind of feels that way."

Kaz shook his head. "The Talents aren't alive—no more than your conscience is alive, or your anger is alive. You may feel like these things have a life to them, but that's dangerous—it makes them external, Al. Like you don't have responsibility for them. Your Talent *is* a piece of you. I have a feeling that if we're going to get the Talents working again, you'll need to understand that."

"I suppose," I said.

"Good. Also, missile."

I leaped for shelter in a ditch as a missile came spiraling down toward us. This one wasn't a dud—it blasted into a nearby hut, and the sound of the explosion nearly deafened me. I looked up, dazed, to find Kaz beside me. A large piece of metal had been thrown by the blast directly into the wall of the ditch not an inch above his head. He looked up at it, measured the distance—quite minuscule—and raised an eyebrow behind his sunglasses toward me.

"Going to tell me how short people are more remarkable than tall people?" I asked, dusting myself off and standing up.

"That's a misunderstanding," Kaz said, leading the way again. "Short people aren't, on average, any more remarkable than taller people. In fact, I'd say that the remarkability in me is about equivalent to the remarkability in you."

"That's very good of you to admit."

"Of course . . . my remarkability *is* packed into a smaller container, so it's more concentrated. Like the difference between lemon juice and citric acid. So my remarkability is more effective, you see."

I snorted. "You're a loon."

"Yes, and fortunately my looniness is also more concentrated, like—"

I held up a hand, stopping him. We'd just turned a corner to look straight at the jail, which was really a small vacation hut with the windows nailed shut and the doors barred from the outside. The Mokians weren't big on actual prison facilities.

A missile had hit beside the structure, blasting open the wall. My mother, if she was still alive, was free.

Chapter

Norton

I wonder why I keep writing these chapter introductions. I spend a lot of time in these stories not actually writing these stories. There must be something to it. Something I don't want to admit.

These are another delay. To keep myself from writing the inevitable. As long as I'm waxing fanciful about bunnies and bazookas, I don't have to make progress toward the ending.

I don't want to get there. Despite claiming I'm writing these autobiographies to set the story straight, I don't actually want to do it. Deep down, I'd rather think of myself as a hero.

Of course, I'm probably too much of a coward to include this section in the book.

I took a deep breath, then stepped up to the improvised prison and peeked through the broken wall. My mother, Shasta Smedry, sat inside on a little stool, reading a book. She wore a plaid skirt and tight vest over a white blouse—typical Librarian clothing—with her blonde hair in a bun. She had on horn-rimmed spectacles and seemed completely unconcerned that a missile had ripped this room in half.

"Ah, there you are," she said, spotting me. "About time. I hope you aren't adopting some of your grandfather's proclivities, Alcatraz."

"Why are you just sitting there?" I asked.

"Where else would I go?"

"You could have escaped."

"I don't want to escape. You are currently my best bet at reaching Attica before he does anything stupid." She stood up and tossed the book aside—a callous act for a Librarian. But then again it was merely a fantasy novel, so nothing that important.

Looking at her felt like getting punched in the gut. I still saw her as Ms. Fletcher—the social worker who had watched over me as a child. She'd been with me through most of my life, and had taken every opportunity to berate me, tear me down, and undermine my every success.

I'd spent my life feeling abandoned, alone, and

worthless—and all the time my mother had been there, never telling me who she was, never offering a moment of comfort. Everything could have gone so differently if this woman had been willing to show me an ounce of kindness.

"Ah, and the brother," Shasta said, glancing at Kaz. "I hope you're not planning on bringing him, Alcatraz. It was to be only us three. You, me, Leavenworth."

"And anyone else you approve."

"Then I don't approve Kazan."

"Fine," I said, meeting my mother's gaze. "Kaz, tell Grandpa to power down the penguin. We're not going anywhere."

Shasta stared back at me, arms folded. "You've changed," she finally said. "You're harder now. I applaud that. Very well, Kazan may join us. Let's be moving."

No matter what situation my mother was in, she always seemed to be able to control it. She even made prison seem like a deliberate choice. Though . . . that might make sense. If you think about it, prison involves free food, a room all to yourself (so long as you are insistent about it), and a bunch of like-minded individuals with whom to make friends. Beyond that, all of the *really* hardcore criminals are too skillful to be caught, so you'll be safe from them inside the prison.

Of course, if you've been doing all the things I tell you

to in these books, you're probably already in prison. To be honest, it's a wonder to me that I haven't spent most of these books locked up myself.*

Mother in tow, we headed back for the landing field. The missiles continued to fall—in fact, one exploded high above us, leaving me confused. Another malfunction? But no—this one dropped little parachutes bearing small, spiderlike machines, each the size of a basketball. These landed, then began to rip apart buildings, attacking them with lasers on their forelegs.

The Librarians knew everyone would evacuate. Now they were going to level the city with robots while the people were all hiding.

"This is what you're part of," I snapped at my mother. "This is what you support."

"Don't be tiresome, Alcatraz. I don't support everything the Librarians do any more than you support everything the Free Kingdoms—and their monarchs—do."

We pulled to a stop as Kaz waved for us to wait beside a broken hut. He looked out, watching a group of spider robots scramble past.

---

* Though as I think about it, my worst legal infraction has been the employment of superfluous footnotes, which is something I only just started doing.

"Yeah?" I whispered to my mother as we waited. "You dress like a Librarian, talk like one. You work with them, and don't speak out against them. You're one of them. And you share responsibility for *this*."

"You think I could simply leave the Hushlands behind? Join the Free Kingdoms?"

"It's what I did."

"Oh, so you're a Free Kingdomer now?" my mother asked. "Do you think like them? Act like them? You don't miss things like hamburgers and blue jeans?"

"I . . ."

"You're not one of them, Alcatraz. A few months of irresponsible playing with your grandfather won't erase a decade and a half of living in the Hushlands. You—"

I couldn't talk to her. I moved as soon as Kaz nodded to us, and I outpaced the other two, angry. It probably wouldn't have hurt so much if it hadn't had a grain of truth to it.

Even still, I didn't know where I belonged. I felt like an outsider in the Free Kingdoms; I rarely understood what was going on or why people did what they did. Yet I certainly didn't miss the Hushlands as much as my mother wanted to imply. Burgers and jeans were great and all, but I'd never be able to live there in peace, knowing what I now knew of the world.

Was I destined to spend my life without a real home? Had anything changed from the days when I'd moved from family to family, like a bad smell through a crowded room?

I hated that my mother could get to me. I hated that she could be wrong, yet still be *just* right enough to get under my skin. Also I hated asparagus. But that's not particularly relevant now, so I'm not sure why I brought it up.

I was charging so quickly that I didn't notice the group of spider things gathering together up ahead, clicking to one another and gesturing at our little group. Kaz cried out, grabbing one of his guns. We were almost back to the landing field—we'd reached the place where that first missile had fallen, but not exploded.

"Lovely," my mother said, stepping up beside me and regarding the bunch of robots. "You threw a tantrum and ran us into *this*. You are still a child, Alcatraz. Don't forget that, just because the Nalhallans are willing to send thirteen-year-old kids into war zones."

"Better than trying to crush their spirits," I said, "letting them think they were orphans. Never telling them who you were."

"Oh? And was your father any better? Your grandfather? At least *I* looked out for you."

"Because you wanted the Sands of Rashid," I said. "Not because you cared about me. You—"

"I'm your *mother*," Shasta said. "You will not speak to me in such a way."

"Uh, guys?" Kaz said. "Robot death army! Guys?"

"You're not my mother," I said. "You're merely the woman who gave birth to me—and I'm surprised you didn't find a surrogate for *that* endeavor! You seem to be content to avoid all the *other* hard work associated with raising a child!"

Shasta folded her arms.

"As for being young," I said, kneeling down, "yeah, I'm aware. Doesn't mean I haven't figured out a few things." I pressed my hand against the unexploded missile on the ground beside us, sending a surge of Oculator energy into it.

The rocket came alive, glowing white, a jet of flame shooting out the back. It burst away from me and slammed into the approaching pack of robots, then *exploded*. The blast was far enough from us that we weren't hurt, but the robots weren't so lucky; it probably sent little bits of them flying as far as Mongolia.

I blinked in shock. I hadn't been expecting the thing to explode; I'd planned for it to push through the robots and make a path. So it hadn't been a dud after all? And I'd knelt down and *touched* the thing?

My mother didn't so much as cringe as the pieces of robots fell around us, and she seemed completely unimpressed by my awesome robot-destroying skills.

"You're as bad as your father," she said.

"So *now* I'm like the Free Kingdomers?" I said, shaken.

"Don't be silly," Shasta said, striding away from me. "Your father never fit in here either. He never fit in anywhere. It's part of what I like about him."

Troubled, I followed until we reached the airfield, which had collected some smoldering holes during our absence. The enormous glass penguin stood in their midst like the last flag flapping on a battlefield, only far dumber-looking.

My grandfather's torso poked out of a window about where the penguin's navel would have been, if it were a glass mammal instead of a glass bird. "Colliding Kowals!" he yelled at us. "What took you so long? Get in, get in! Oh, and by the way, Shasta, I'm giving this penguin to you!"

"Giving it to me?" she shouted up at him as we reached the base of the penguin. "Why in the world would you do that?"

"Because I promised my grandson we'd steal a ship to ride out," Grandpa yelled back, "and we can't very well do that if we own the blasted thing. So it's yours.

Incidentally, we're stealing it. Onward!" He pulled back into the penguin.

Kaz led us up a stairway into the base of the penguin. Within, the vehicle consisted of lots of steps and small rooms off to the sides. An elevator would have been lovely, but Free Kingdomers have this strange idea about steps being more advanced than something like elevators. Don't ask me to explain it again—it really doesn't make much sense.

After a lot of climbing, we reached the head of the penguin, where the eyes acted like a windshield for us to look out of. "Welcome to *Penguinator!*" Grandpa said from a bucket seat next to a window.

"*Penguinator?*" Shasta said flatly.

"Named it myself!" Grandpa said.

"I couldn't tell." Shasta settled down in one of the seats, and Kaz took the seat nearest the eye-windows. He'd be our pilot. He flipped some switches and the entire vessel rattled, a hum coming from down below.

I remained standing, leaning back against a glass wall. I'd come to Mokia in a flash, on a quest equal parts determination and desperation. I'd barely gotten to see the place, despite wearing its crown, and now I was off again.

That was my life. I'd only been in Nalhalla for a few

months before leaving for Mokia, and now I was off back to the Hushlands.

Where *did* I belong?

Penguinator vibrated more violently. The way Free Kingdomer vehicles worked, the entire thing was made of glass, but it wasn't a hundred percent transparent.

"Alcatraz?" Kaz asked. "You going to sit down?"

"I think I'll stand."

"Might not be safe," Kaz said, pulling a lever. The vehicle shook as an explosion came from nearby. Missiles were still falling on the city.

"We going to rock a lot as we waddle to the ocean?" I asked, settling down in a glass seat.

"Waddle?" Grandpa asked. "Don't tell me you believe Librarian penguin propaganda."

"Flightless sea fowl?" I asked. "Adorable and silly? I've seen them at zoos."

"Those are the juveniles," Grandpa said. "Not fully grown."

"Uh . . . and what are the adults like?"

The entire room rotated unexpectedly; the penguin's head was turning up toward the sky.

Something rumbled down below.

"Well," Grandpa said, "we've tried to replicate their biological jet boosters. Unfortunately, we haven't ever been able to match their natural airspeed. But I believe they *were* the original inspiration that made Librarian scientists create the first rockets."

"That's—"

The rest of what I was going to say was lost as the giant glass penguin exploded out of Mokia and shot into the air.

Chapter

Bob

I admit nothing.

You might say that my dialogue in these books sounds too heroic at times to be real. "Alcatraz," you say to me, "real people, particularly teenagers, don't say things like 'You're merely the woman who gave birth to me—and I'm surprised you didn't find a surrogate for *that* endeavor.'" To which I reply, "Stop reading over my shoulder as I type. And how did you get into my house anyway?"

I've told you before, and I guess I need to reiterate, that everything in these biographies is one hundred percent true and not altered in any way. Yes, a real teenage boy talking to his mother might have said, "Uh, you're stupid. And stuff." Fortunately, *I'm* far more eloquent.

And if you don't believe me, well, uh, you're stupid. And stuff.

Penguinator's blastoff shoved me back in my seat. I could practically feel my skin pulling back from my mouth and eyes as we zoomed upward. Missiles fell around us, trailing smoke, but somehow—whether by luck or clever flying—we missed colliding with any of them. I was quite pleased by that fact. I hate exploding so early in the day.*

Kaz let out a whoop as we streaked away from Mokia. I let out a gurgle that was meant as a cross between a philosophic representation of my disgust for all things Librarian and a wish that I'd thought to use the bathroom before climbing aboard.

Eventually the machine leveled out in the sky, turning horizontal like a jet plane—a giant glass jet plane shaped like a penguin with a large flame shooting out of its butt. These are the kinds of classy moments the Librarians try to prevent you from reading, kids.

"What are we looking at for the flight time?" Grandpa asked once we'd leveled out.

"Maybe an hour," Kaz said.

---

* Being blown up is definitely more of an afternoon thing.

I checked the clock on the dashboard. That would put us at about one in the afternoon when the Librarian defenses around Washington, DC, blew us up. Much better.

"Any ideas on how we're going to get in?" Kaz asked.

"Something will come up," Grandpa said cheerfully.

"You always say things like that," Draulin said. "Color me skeptical."

"Could you get us in?" I asked my mother.

"Not a chance," she said. "They don't trust me. Haven't in years. They're not going to let me into the Highbrary."

"Disguiser's Lenses, then," I said. "They can make us look like anyone else. Grandpa and I can put them on, and imitate important Librarians."

"You think the Librarians aren't ready for something like that?" my mother asked. "The Highbrary isn't some simple local branch; it has protections in place. Defenses. Anytime an Oculator uses one of their Lenses inside the place, they glow brightly. You'll never be able to use one for a disguise."

"She's right," Draulin said. "That has always prevented us from being able to sneak in."

"Well," Kaz said, "maybe we could crash *Penguinator* as a distraction. We throw out some lifelike dummies to enhance the illusion that we're all dead. You might work for one of those, Draulin. How dedicated are you to the Smedry cause?"

Draulin gave my uncle a very stern look, the type only she can—

Wait, *Draulin?*

Yes, that was her. Bastille's mother, decked out in plate armor, Crystin sword strapped to her back. She had a severe haircut, a more severe face, and an even *more* severe temperament.

Draulin, like her daughter, was a knight sworn to protect my family line. That didn't explain why she was here, standing by the doorway, arms folded.

"Uh," I asked, looking at the others, "isn't anyone else surprised that she's suddenly here?"

"Nah," Grandpa said. "Draulin has been doing this for years."

She narrowed her eyes at Grandpa. "When I heard young Smedry's proclamation to the Librarians, I realized you were likely going to try to sneak away."

Shattering Glass. Had the *entire city* seen my little show for the monarchs?

"I easily determined you'd take this ship," Draulin said, "as it is the fastest and most elegant in the Smedry fleet. Do you have any idea how *difficult* it is to guard you people when you never tell us where you're going?"

"Obviously," Grandpa said in his perky way. "Otherwise we wouldn't do it!" He smiled at Draulin.

"Irresponsible troublemaker," Draulin said.

"Stick-in-the-mud."

"Detestable threat to peace."

"*Tu'mi'kapi*."

"That's a new one."

"It means 'old bat' in Mokian."

"Ah."

"A term of endearment, of course."

"Among bats, perhaps," Draulin said, settling herself into a seat with a clink.

I watched the exchange with befuddlement. Despite their words, the two seemed genuinely fond of one another, a sense I'd never gotten before. I mean, Draulin couldn't possibly be fond of anything, could she?*

"I'm not sure what to be more offended by, Old Smedry," Draulin said, perched in her seat in a way that didn't look at all comfortable. "That you'd go on a mission with a notorious Librarian agent without telling me, or that you'd leave for the *one place* where we can find a cure for my daughter's ailment and not think to invite me to help."

---

* Other than, you know, eating bricks, glaring at passersby, and winning growling contests.

"I figured you'd have more fun sneaking aboard," Grandpa said. "Just like old times!"

"Old times were miserable."

"Exactly the sort of thing you enjoy, then!"

Her lips—amazingly—tugged upward at the corners, as if she were *smiling*. And back in Nalhalla, she'd almost seemed to display an affection for her family. Maybe I'd overestimated this woman's sternness.

Draulin reached out sideways with a sudden motion and punched my mother in the face with a gauntleted hand.

I stared in disbelief as Shasta was thrown off her seat by the punch. She rolled on the floor, but came up on one knee, hair mussed, glasses askew. All in all, she looked rather *not dead* for having been punched by a Knight of Crystallia.

"Stuttering Silverbergs!" Grandpa exclaimed, leaping from his seat. "Draulin, that was uncalled-for."

"Be calm," Draulin said, standing and meeting my mother's gaze. "She's obviously wearing some kind of protective glass. I needed to measure its damage capacity."

"But still!" Grandpa looked from Draulin to Shasta.

My mother stood up calmly and straightened her glasses. "And *I* am supposed to be the 'evil' one? What if I hadn't had a protective field, knight?"

"Then you'd be unconscious," Draulin said. "And we'd all be safer." She looked away from Shasta and stepped up next to Kaz at the glass control panel, then reached underneath it and pulled out a small device with a blinking light. She held it up, spinning on Shasta. "Did any of you see her plant this?"

I gawked, then looked at my mother. "How did you manage *that*?"

"I obviously didn't," Shasta said, folding her arms. "It's a Librarian tracking device, but it's not mine. I don't know how it got there."

I wished I could read Shasta. She said everything with the same passionless voice. To her, getting punched in the face seemed about as distracting as having a fly land on her knee.*

Draulin crushed the device in her fist. "As usual, you Smedrys have no idea what you're getting yourselves into."

"Oh, we know," I said. "We just don't care."

Draulin gave me a glare that could have burned toast.

"I did not plant that bug," Shasta said, settling back down on her seat. "And Leavenworth, if you wish my aid

---

* As for me, I'd consider getting punched in the face to be about as annoying as being constantly forced to read footnotes that don't add anything to the narrative.

on this mission of yours, then you'll keep your watch-
dog more carefully leashed." She fished in her pocket and
brought out a thin disc of glass that had cracked down the
center. Whatever protective field she maintained, Draulin
had done it some serious damage.

"Draulin," Grandpa said, "no more punching things
unless I give you the go-ahead."

She regarded him with a raised eyebrow.

"And no more kicking them, attacking them with
swords or other weapons, head-butting them, or body-
slamming them."

"Very well."

"No biting either," Grandpa added.

Draulin's face fell visibly. "Watch that one," she said,
pointing at Shasta. "We need to be extra careful on this
mission. My daughter's safety is at stake. I want to have
the cure in hand as soon as possible so that she can be
revived to help us."

". . . Help us?" I asked. "You *brought* Bastille?"

"Of course I did," Draulin said. "I will need her aid
dealing with three"—she glanced at my mother—"well,
technically *four* Smedrys. Bastille is below, in the infir-
mary."

"Delightful," Shasta said. "So you won't have anyone to

blame but yourself when your daughter gets killed alongside everyone else on this mission."

Draulin stood up with a clinking of armor.

"Ahem," Grandpa said. "Draulin, why don't you go search the rest of the ship for more tracking devices?"

Draulin glared at Shasta, then faced Grandpa and bowed. "Yes, Lord Smedry," she said before turning and marching from the room. I was a little surprised she obeyed; Bastille would have told him to shove the order up his mustache.

Not wanting to be near my mother any longer, I rose to follow Draulin. I didn't have any specific plans for where I was going, but my grandfather piped up. "Your quarters are on deck three, Alcatraz. Technically this is part of your fleet—or it was, until I gave it to Shasta—so you should have a wardrobe in your closet. I'd suggest changing. That bathrobe isn't appropriate unless you have a towel too."

Walking through the inside of *Penguinator* proved to be an odd experience, now that the entire ship was turned horizontal. To go between "floors," Draulin and I had to enter the stairwells and walk along a pathway beside the steps. Had *all* the rooms been built so you could walk on both the floor and the wall?

We passed a window, and I stopped in place. Were those *penguins* shooting through the air beside us? Real ones, not made of glass, each with a large flame jetting from their posterior?

"Penguins?" I asked, pointing.

"Giant penguins," Draulin said, sounding distracted.

"They really can fly?"

"Of course," Draulin said. "Why else would they look like missiles?"

I shook my head. Every time I thought I understood the world, something like this dropped on me like—well—a giant penguin.* I hurried on, and though I spotted a sign on the wall saying we'd reached deck three, I followed Draulin for another two decks. Here she entered a glass room.

Bastille was strapped to a bed. It looked like the chamber was built to rotate when the penguin took off—which matched some other Free Kingdomer technology I'd seen, so I wasn't surprised. Draulin began searching the room for bugs or tracking devices, peering under tables and glass shelves.

I walked to Bastille. She looked so . . . helpless. Her

---

* Stupid giant penguins.

mother had dressed her in simple pajamas, like what we wear in the Hushlands, and her sword was strapped to the table next to her. Her silver hair was spread out around her head, her eyes closed. Someone else might have looked peaceful, but looking at her, all I could do was imagine how angry she'd be.

It's not right, I thought. *Bastille shouldn't be an invalid.*

Was there anything more I could do, other than hunt down the cure? What would Bastille have wanted me to do, if she could talk?

Honestly, she'd probably have wanted me to punch anyone who mentioned her being helpless.

"I couldn't leave her," Draulin said, stepping up beside me. "The missiles were falling, and I knew you and your grandfather would be sneaking away. I grabbed Bastille, but I didn't have time to get to one of the shelters. The only thing to do was to bring her, you see. I . . ."

"It's okay," I said.

"I've been too hard on her," Draulin said. She'd taken off one of her gauntlets, and she laid her hand on Bastille's cheek in a tender motion. "I so wanted her to follow her father's path, not mine. The life of a knight is a lonely one."

She almost seemed to be tearing up. It was like seeing a rock cry. I watched, baffled.

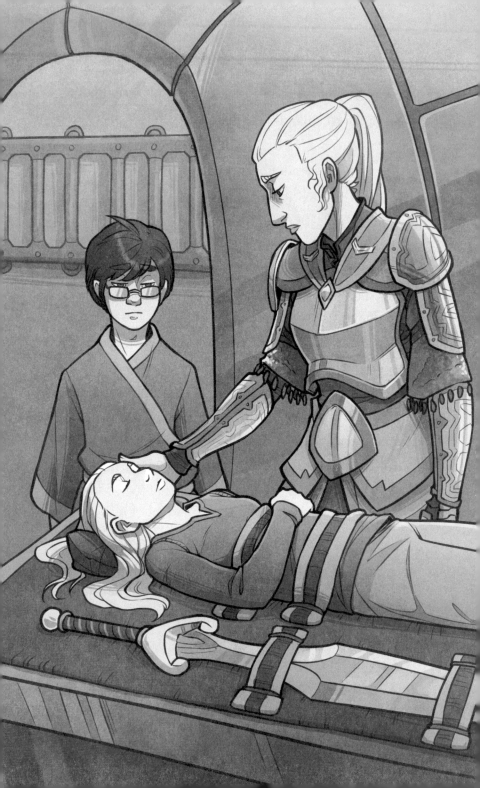

So that's what it's like to have a parent who actually cares, I thought. *Huh.*

"So helpless," Draulin said.

I punched her.

"Lord Smedry?" she asked, looking at me as I shook my hand. Punching people wearing plate mail armor = not smart.

"That was for her," I said. "Because she'd be mad . . . er . . . you see, I figured that she would want . . ."

"Ah," Draulin said. "Of course. That makes sense."

Draulin continued her search for tracking devices, and I eventually made my way back up to deck three, where my quarters were marked with my name. I could turn the walls dark by touching them and giving a command, so I could catch a nap if I wanted—or change clothing without worrying that I'd reflect something unmentionable* all the way up to the cockpit.

I darkened the walls, then looked in the closet, where I found a nice selection of clothing. Most was of Free Kingdomer make—Mokian wraps, Nalhallan tunics, that sort of thing. On one side, however, a series of Hushlander outfits hung on hooks. There were a few T-shirts, and

---

* My bum.

even a pair of jeans, along with some more abnormal costumes. Free Kingdomers had some odd ideas about what
people wore in the Hushlands—a lot of their views of us
came from fashion magazines and old movies they stole.

I found a note pinned to one T-shirt.

*I've gathered clothing of a wide variety, useful in a potential
infiltration. However, I don't believe for a moment that
Hushlanders actually wear things so bland as this Twee-
Shirt. I'd suggest against this, and instead would wear the
chicken costume I've hung at the back.*

—Janie

When in the world had she found time to stock this
chamber? I shook my head, tucking away the note. I
grabbed a T-shirt and jeans, then walked to the bed—
which was not glass, fortunately—and prepared to
dress.

I found myself sitting there, however, holding the
clothing. All through my adventures, I'd stubbornly worn
my Hushlander garb. It was familiar; it was comfortable.
It was *me*, wasn't it?

I looked back at the closet. Should I wear a tunic
instead?

You're not one of them, Alcatraz. . . .

I hated that my mother was right. I debated for far too long. Then something in the closet* caught my eye, and I couldn't help but smile.

A short time later I approached the cockpit of *Penguinator*, a conversation between my grandfather and Kaz drifting out and echoing in the hallway.

"We can't get to Sing Sing," Kaz was saying. "There's just not enough time."

"We need an expert, Son," Grandpa said. "I don't know the Hushlands nearly well enough, and young Alcatraz grew up in one little town. I'm telling you, our team isn't complete. We need someone else."

"But Dif?" Kaz asked. "You know how little I like *him*."

"Oh, he's not so bad."

"He's *weird*," Kaz said.

I walked up to the doorway. "He must be pretty strange indeed," I said, "if he's weird in comparison to *us*."

The two turned toward me. My mother still sat in her seat, reading a book she'd pulled out of her pocket. She glanced toward me, and her jaw dropped visibly.

I wore a tuxedo—complete with red bow tie—matching my grandfather's. It was ridiculous. He wore the clothing

---

* No, not the chicken suit, you sadist.

because he assumed that it would help him blend into the Hushlands, but it actually made him stand out.

To me that clothing represented something. I pulled out a pair of reddish-tinted Oculator's Lenses and slipped them on. I might not fit in with the Hushlanders or with the average Free Kingdomer, but there *was* a place I fit.

I was a Smedry.

Chapter

Lilliana

How dramatic. Let's talk about Aesop.

Oh, I'm sorry. Were you expecting the book to continue on with my daring infiltration of the Highbrary? Great. That means you have something to look forward to.

Aesop was a funny little Greek man known for his love of animal puppets, for his fondness for jumping off cliffs* without parachutes, and for maybe never existing in the first place. (Like Socrates, the guy really should have learned to write stuff down.)

Aesop was a storyteller who shamelessly used fictional

---

* Well, *one* cliff at least.

characters in clever narrative to insult and make fun of the people listening to his stories. So basically he was the most awesome person ever. If he were still alive, I'd have asked him to write my autobiography for me. Unfortunately, see the line about cliffs above.

Anyway, there's a theme running through all the stories Aesop told: If you're in one, you're probably doomed. Whether you be a frog (eaten by a heron), a grasshopper (starved to death in the winter), a snake (pinched to death by his best friend the crab), a deer (heart eaten by a lion), or a mouse (suffocated inside an oyster, seriously), life is shown to be short, while death is depicted as brutal and often humiliating.

I've noticed something about these stories as we retell them. They're getting nicer. In modern incarnations, the grasshopper doesn't starve but is taken in by the ants. (Likewise, modern fairy tales involve fewer girls turning into sea foam, and more singing crabs.)

Why is this important? Well, I'll tell you.*

Eventually.

"So who is this Dif guy?" I asked, leaning against the wall and folding my arms. I felt suave wearing a tuxedo. If

---

* As if you had any doubt.

you've never tried it, you really should. Then I can laugh at you for looking so ridiculous because there's no way you'll pull this off as well as I do.

"Dif is a Smedry cousin," Grandpa said. "He checked in a few minutes ago, and it occurred to me that I needed someone else for the team. He's spent most of his life embedded deeply inside the Hushlands, and is one of our foremost experts on Librarian culture."

"He's a loon," Kaz said.

"He's family."

"So is Shasta, Pop."

My mother sniffed from the back of the room, turning a page in another book she'd pulled out from somewhere.

"How's he related?" I asked. I still hadn't quite figured out the family tree.

"My uncle's son," Grandpa said. "His family was part of a deep infiltration in the Hushlands for decades; the Librarians eventually found them, but he escaped. He's got a powerful Talent—or rather he *had* one, before your intervention. Look, Kaz, Dif has spent a lifetime in the Hushlands. And he's nearby, at the Worldspire, doing research."

"I know," Kaz grumbled. "He has this annoying habit of calling me and telling me all about what he's had for breakfast."

"Excellent!" Grandpa said. "We'll swing by and pick him up."

The Worldspire? I slipped into Grandpa's seat as he wandered off to find the facilities.* The Worldspire was where Crystin knights, like Bastille and Draulin, got the gemstones that gave them superhuman powers. The things were stuck in the back of their necks and did some other weird stuff too, connecting them all together. I'm not sure exactly what it all means—the third book was a bit confusing to me in that regard.

Kaz, muttering under his breath, used the dashboard to give this Dif fellow a call. The voice on the other side was energetic and high-pitched. Kaz had the volume way down, so I couldn't hear much, but it seemed like Dif was very excited to be invited on the mission.

Reluctantly, Kaz adjusted the controls and turned *Penguinator*'s flight path a few degrees. Grandpa, who had returned by this point, patted him on the shoulder. "I'm going to go get our Lenses ready," he then said to me. "I've packed quite the arsenal for us. Come down to my room once you've met Cousin Dif, and I can go over them for you."

It wasn't long before I caught sight of the Worldspire

---

* AKA the poopin' place. Aren't you so glad you read these footnotes?

jutting up out of the ocean ahead. When I'd first seen it months ago, it had been very distant. I'd thought it looked like a tower, and I was close to right—but it was more an enormous crystal. It reminded me of Bastille's sword, except in the shape of a very thin mountain.

I hadn't expected it to be populated, but as we drew closer I could see a city built at its base and wooden scaffolding wrapping up, up, up and around the entire thing.

"For studying it?" I asked, pointing.

Kaz nodded. "The Worldspire is one of the world's great mysteries. Though the Crystin don't talk about their stones much, their powers ultimately come from a chunk of that spire. You know that odd ringing you get in your ears sometimes?"

"Yeah?"

"That happens when someone taps the Worldspire on its tip. Tap it, and a random number of people all through-out the world will get a ringing sensation."

"Huh."

"That's not the only thing," Kaz said. "Cold chills? Because a wind blows on the Worldspire. Unexplained headache? Something struck the spire. What happens to the spire is transferred to a random number of people, different ones each time."

"That's . . . kind of creepy."

"Well, it's certainly odd. We're all connected somehow, and that crystal is in the center of it."

Now, if you've been paying attention to what I've been writing in these books up until this point, you might have recognized that conversation as foreshadowing. Well done! Except you're wrong.

Oh, this *would* be foreshadowing if my autobiography were going to go beyond this final book. But it's not.* Besides, you don't need me to tell you what happened there. Even in the Hushlands, events involving the Worldspire would have been hard to ignore. Go ask your parents. They lived through it.

If, when you ask them, your parents act like they don't know what you're talking about, one of three things is going on.

1. Your parents are Librarian spies. (Whereupon you should eat some of their cookies as a sign of rebellion against Librarian oppression.)
2. Your parents had their minds wiped by a Librarian memory-erasing toad. (The most likely answer.

---

* For once, I'm not even lying here.

This often leaves the person a little absentminded as a side effect, so you should be able to swipe a cookie without them noticing.)

3. Your parents are just dumb. (If that's the case, have a cookie to console yourself. I'm sure it's not hereditary or anything. Also, stop chewing on that phone case. It's not a cookie.)

Penguinator approached the Worldspire. And didn't slow down.

"Uh . . ." I said. I hadn't realized exactly how fast we were going. "Shouldn't we . . ."

"In too much of a hurry to stop," Kaz said, pulling a glass lever. "See that cage over there?"

A large metal cage had been set out, hanging from a pole that extended from some scaffolding around the Worldspire. I barely had time to spot it before we zipped past. *Penguinator* shook. A second later the Worldspire was a large shadow retreating behind us, visible reflected through the glass walls.

"I extended a hook on a rope," Kaz explained, moving the lever again. "Hit the cage and pulled it along. Maybe."

"I'm not even going to ask about things like sudden acceleration, whiplash, or the laws of conservation of momentum."

"Good," Kaz said. "You're learning."

Free Kingdomers have this habit of pretending the laws of physics don't exist. For the most part it works, as evidenced by the arrival of Dif. He burst into the cockpit, bucktoothed and grinning, a man in his fifties wearing suspenders, a bow tie, and enough plaid to outfit an entire Scottish clan.*

"An infiltration!" Dif exclaimed. "With Kaz and Leavenworth, two of my favorite people!" He whooped, then ran over and hugged Kaz around the back of the chair.

Kaz groaned softly; he looked like he'd eaten a fish stick.

"And Cousin Alcatraz himself!" Dif said, standing upright and spinning on me. I raised my hands to prevent a hug.

I got one anyway.

"Uh, hi," I said from the embrace. "What's your Talent, Cousin Dif?" I'd learned this was the proper way to introduce oneself to a member of the family.

I expected something relating to making people

---

* Seriously. He wore plaid pants of one pattern, a plaid shirt of a second pattern, and a bow tie of a *third*. It looked so bad, I figured at first he must be a retired monarch, as nobody would dress that way intentionally.

uncomfortable, like Aunt Pattywagon. Instead, Dif pulled back and, with a big grin, said, "I'm really forgetful!"

"Librarian memory-erasing toad?" I asked.

"No, not at all!" Dif said. "For me it's natural."

"It's a quite powerful Talent," Kaz said grudgingly. "It can affect everyone around him. Only three people in the history of the Smedry line have had it."

"Cool," I said, smiling as Dif nodded. I didn't get what made Kaz so uptight about the guy. Yes, he was . . . enthusiastic, but so were most Smedrys. "Like you can make people forget that you were spotted, and things like that?"

"I have no idea," Dif said, grinning.

"Every time he uses his Talent, everyone immediately forgets about it," Kaz explained.

"That sounds inconvenient."

Dif shrugged. "Like breaking things by accident? Or getting lost when you don't intend to?"

I nodded. It wouldn't be a Smedry Talent without bizarre side effects. "But . . . how do you know what your Talent can do if you can't remember using it?"

"It comes to me when I need it. Like this morning. I can't remember at all what happened to me right after breakfast! Means my Talent engaged."

"This morning?" Kaz asked. "Your Talent *worked*?"

"Sure did," Dif said. He looked from Kaz to me. "Is . . . that a problem?"

"Not a problem," Kaz said, rubbing his chin, "but maybe a clue. Eh, Al?"

I nodded slowly. It might mean the Talents were still working sporadically . . . or maybe Dif had been far enough away that his Talent never got broken. Or maybe he was simply forgetful by nature, and his Talent had nothing to do with what had happened this morning. I had no way to tell; I'd have to watch him and see if it happened again.

"I should go see what Lenses Grandpa has for me," I said.

"Great!" Dif said. "That'll be awesowambastic!"

". . . What?" I asked.

"Awesowambastic!" Dif said. "It's a word I just made up. It means exactly as awesome as we all are!" He grabbed me with one arm in a buddylike side hug. "Smedrys, am I right?"

"Okay, sure," I said, extricating myself.

"Be quick if you can, Al," Kaz said, reading some numbers on his glass control panel. "We've got under a half hour before we hit the Librarian defenses outside Washington, DC."

"I'm guessing this ship doesn't have any weapons on it," I said with a sigh. "They never seem to—"

"Look at my ant farm!" Dif said, lifting up a glass-sided thin box and setting it on the dashboard between us.

"Uh . . ." I said.

Yes. An ant farm. Where had he been *hiding* the thing?

"It's a metaphor," Dif said, leaning down to look at the ants. "I gave them little machine guns."

"What does it have to do with what we're talking about now?" I asked.

"Nothing!" Dif said. "That's the beauty of it. Interruptions are great attention-grabbers. The wackier and more

bizarre, the better! 'Cuz we're Smedrys! Awesowambas-
ticly so! Right guys? Right?" He shook the ant farm to get
the ants moving more quickly. Fortunately they seemed
to be completely ignoring the little toy machine guns he'd
dropped in.

I stared at Dif for an extended moment. Nearby, my
mother seemed to be stifling laughter as she turned the
next page in her book.

And suddenly I found myself hating Dif with a raw,
insidious passion. It was completely unfair, completely
uncharitable, and completely beneath me.* I felt it
anyway.

I shoved down the emotion, ashamed. Why should I
hate Dif? He was a little eccentric, but so were we all. We
were . . . Smedrys . . . and . . .

Were the rest of us this bad?

Uncomfortable, I left him explaining the convoluted
metaphor of his weaponized ant farm to Kaz.

Hopefully I was about to get weaponized myself.

---

* Like pretty much everything else at the moment, considering how I
was flying and all.

Mary

Now that we're all annoyed at my annoying cousin, let me remind you that this is not a fable. Aesop didn't write this story. Life did, and there isn't always a point to life. Sometimes it simply *is*. My experiences aren't a neat package with a pithy moral at the end.

That said, I've been pretty fixated on fables and fairy tales lately. The old ones are dark, dark, dark—yet the ones we tell ourselves these days always seem to need a happy ending. Go browse your bookstore. How many stories there end with the protagonist being eaten by a fox? None, I'd bet. Instead the endings involve marriages, parties, or kisses. Often all three.

Why are we different now? Is it because the Librarians are protecting us from stories with sad endings? Or is it something about who we are, who we have become as a society, that makes us need to see the good guys win?

We seem to crave proof that it can happen.

I trailed into my grandfather's quarters in the ship. He'd marked the door with a bow tie. Kooky and individualistic, just like a Smedry should be, right?

Inside, Grandpa sat at a glass table, polishing his Lenses. He'd set them out before him in two double rows. "You met Cousin Dif?" he asked as I stepped up beside him.

"Yeah."

He put the final Lenses down and tucked away his polishing cloth. "Don't be too hard on the lad, Alcatraz," Grandpa said. "He wants to fit in with us, and perhaps he tries a little too hard. He's had a difficult life. It is good to show him kindness, and he really is quite knowledgeable."

I didn't reply, but to me Grandpa's words seemed off. It wasn't that Dif didn't fit in. It was like . . . well, Dif seemed to fit in *too* well. Like a finger in a nostril.

Grandpa took a Lens with his finger and slid it across the table toward me. My Truthfinder's Lens. The next one was of a purple and green tint; the single remaining Bestower's Lens my grandfather had lent me. It had a big crack straight down the center. When I'd fallen unconscious at the end of the siege of Tuki Tuki, apparently I'd dropped the thing, ruining it.

"I'm sorry," I said.

"Well, they *are* made of glass!" Grandpa said. "We can get this one melted down and remade. Don't worry." He debated for a moment, then slid a different Lens toward me. It was a deep maroon, and looked pretty cool—at the very least it wasn't pink or baby blue or anything like that.

I took it and held it up. "Let me guess," I said, "this shows me something important about the world, helping me gain a better appreciation for life and those around me."

"Nope," Grandpa said. "It blows stuff up."

I started. "What, really?"

"Indeed."

"But . . . I mean . . ." While I'd had offensive Lenses before, Grandpa usually didn't think much of them. He preferred Lenses that were about information, as he claimed that knowledge was true power.

"We are heading into the Highbrary," Grandpa said, uncharacteristically subdued. "You'll need to be able to defend yourself. The Shamefiller's Lens is crude, but sometimes crude solutions are most effective. A monocular Lens; I don't have two of those. You are growing skilled enough to properly use Lenses for just one eye."

I smiled, tucking the Lens into the pocket of my tuxedo jacket. "Why is it called a Shamefiller's Lens?"

"Well, it makes the subject really embarrassed before they explode."

I chuckled, then looked at my grandfather. He was serious.*

"So it only works on people," I said.

"What?" Grandpa said. "Of course not. That's very sapientist of you, Alcatraz. I expected better of my grandson, yes I did!"

"I . . ." I frowned, looking at him. "You made that word up, didn't you?"

"Simply try the Lens on something and you'll see. Something far away, mind you, and not too valuable unless it belongs to someone annoying." He tapped the table. "I debated a long time whether to give this to you, as it is so dangerous."

"I'll be careful with it," I said, patting my pocket.

"What? No, not that one. That one's for fun. I mean the next Lens I'm going to give you, the *truly* dangerous one." He selected a Lens off the table. It had a spray of silver-white flakes in it, like the stars of a galaxy. He held it up before him appraisingly.

"What is it?" I asked.

---

* At that moment. Not as a general rule.

"Shaper's Lens," Grandpa said. "It lets you see someone's heart, soul, and innermost desires."

I raised an eyebrow. That was more like the type of Lens I'd been expecting. "An odd name as well."

"I suspect it was deliberate," Grandpa said, his face reflecting in the Lens. "Though Shaper's Lenses can be unpredictable, an Oculator who holds one has great power over others. We are to use its abilities to inspire, to build up, to create. Not to tear down." Grandpa proffered it.

I took the Lens carefully, feeling a little of Grandpa's reverence, although it (still) didn't seem as strong to me as one that made nice explosions.

"This gives you an advantage over others," Grandpa said, "that maybe you should never have. You gain access to the hearts and dreams of those around you, Alcatraz. Do not abuse that knowledge, even against Librarians."

"I'll try."

"There is no Try."

"Excuse me?"

"Try," Grandpa said. "The city. Blasted Librarians captured the thing and renamed it Dumptopia. Anyway, I trust you, lad. That's why I gave you the Lens, after all! Just . . . do be careful, all right? Actually, be careful with *all* Lenses."

"I'm always careful," I said, tucking the Lenses away.

"Be extra careful. Lenses are acting strange. I charged one a few minutes ago, and it released *far* more energy than I'd expected."

"Really?" I said. "So it's not only me. You charge glass more powerfully now too."

"Yes," he said, handing me a last set of Lenses—a pair of Courier's Lenses that would let us chat over distances. "Whatever happened with you and the Talents in Mokia was more . . . far-reaching than we had assumed."

I sat, thoughtful. (Well, technically I was more bloodful than anything else. But there were a few thoughts in there too, along with a Mokian breakfast burrito.) Shortly thereafter, I heard clinking outside. Draulin knocked politely—even though the door was open—and then entered as Grandpa called for her.

"Did you finish—"
Grandpa began.

Draulin gestured wildly and put a hand to her lips. She was apparently worried there was a Librarian listening device of some sort in the room.

"—learning to belly dance?" Grandpa finished.

Belly dance? I mouthed at him.

Had to think fast, he mouthed back.

"I . . ." Draulin gave my grandfather a suffering look. "Did."

"Excellent!" Grandpa said. "And you belly danced in every room of the ship so far?"

"All but this one," Draulin said.

"Well, on with it then!" Grandpa said.

Draulin clinked around the room, searching in glass closets and under glass counters, checking for bugs. I leaned back in my chair as Grandpa picked up his remaining Lenses to stow them.

"I have to say," Grandpa noted, "that's some of the most awful belly dancing I've ever seen."

"Hard to do in full armor," Draulin said, kneeling by our table. She looked up at us and pointed at the bottom of the table.

Sure enough, as I peeked down I found a small Librarian device stuck there. Draulin took a paper from the counter and wrote on it.

Shall I destroy it as I did the others?

Feels like a waste, Grandpa wrote back. *Shouldn't we be able to use it?*

What type of technology is it? I wrote. *Is there glass involved?*

Grandpa looked at Draulin.

The others had a bit of glass in them, she wrote. *Probably Communicator's Glass, set to transmit only one way.*

Grandpa looked at me, raising an eyebrow.* I'd used the glass in the palace to look at the monarchs when they hadn't wanted me to. Could I do the same thing here?

I shrugged. Maybe?

"My, Draulin," Grandpa said loudly—and in a rather fake way. "That's quite a vigorous dance. You should be more careful, otherwise you might faint."†

She gave him a glare that could have steamed some broccoli to go with my toast. Then she started jumping up and down to make her armor clank before finally dropping to the ground with a clatter.

"Oh my!" Grandpa said. "I warned her."

"You sure did."

"Here, let us get down and see if we can make her more comfortable."

The point of all this was, it seemed, to give us an excuse

---

* His own, fortunately.
† Ah, the old faint feint.

to climb down under the table and make noise there. The Librarians were, after all, probably listening in. Grandpa rubbed his chin, looking at the little device on the bottom of the table.

Draulin took out a knife, then used it to carefully pry the metal casing off the bug. Inside we found a small tangle of wires and a very conspicuous piece of glass. Another Librarian device mixing Hushlander technology with glass.

The other two looked at me, so I reached up and touched the glass. For what happened next, I'll refer you to the description a few chapters ago, with emotion-whales and whatnot. I'm not sure I can top that—though this time I did feel an emotion not unlike how a piece of cheddar feels as it turns into a cheese sandwich.

I blinked, holding my finger in place and opening my eyes as voices came through the device. They were very soft, but audible.

"How should I know why they are so intent on making the poor woman dance?" a voice said. "Nothing those people do makes any sense to me!"

"It seems to be some kind of punishment," another said. "They're always complaining about their bodyguards; this must be a type of petty revenge."

"Keep records of everything they do, in detail," another

voice said, female. "The Scrivener will be able to read more into their motives than you will."

I recognized that voice. She Who Cannot Be Named,* a high-up Librarian we'd faced in Nalhalla.

Recognizing the voice was a big enough shock. But that second part stopped me dead.

The Scrivener?

I grew cold immediately. The Scrivener was Biblioden, right? The guy who had come up with the whole "Evil Librarian" thing in the first place? He was dead.

Wasn't he?

"They've grown silent," a Librarian said. "Why is the glass glowing like that? I—"

The glass on our side started to steam, and I yelped, pulling my hand back swiftly as it melted in a glob that dropped and splatted to the floor.

"That's inconvenient," Draulin said, as if I'd melted it on purpose or something.

"Did they say . . . the Scrivener?" I asked.

"Yes," Grandpa said, rubbing his chin.

---

* It's not that saying her name does anything specific, it's just that the name is so difficult to say, few people can manage it. And . . . wow, did I just put something useful in a footnote? I need to be careful not to make a habit of this. Um . . . Rutabaga?

"I have a question," Draulin said.

"So, maybe they picked a new leader?" I said quickly, cutting her off. "And that Librarian is using the title of Scrivener now."

"No other Librarian has ever dared use the title," Grandpa said, "though centuries have passed since Biblioden vanished. The closest is the order of the Scrivener's Bones, who claim to follow his teachings the most vigilantly."

"My question remains," Draulin said.

"When you say . . . vanished," I said to Grandpa, "you mean died, right?"

"Sure, yes," Grandpa said. "Died." He laughed.

"Let me guess," I said. "Nobody knows where he was buried."

"No."

"Great."

"Question . . ."

"Yes, yes, Draulin."

"Can we get off the floor?"

"If you want to be boring, I suppose."

"I personally would like to know how to spit well."

The other two looked at me as we stood up—because yes, we'd had that entire conversation under the table and so what?—and Grandpa frowned at me. "What did you say?"

"Sorry," I said. "I just wanted to make a sentence that was a little bit longer than what you'd said, so the conversation will look cool on the page when I write it down."

"Ah, well, that makes sense."

"Uh . . . guys?" Kaz's face appeared on Grandpa's wall. "You're going to want to come up here. Because we've arrived, and a *shockingly* large number of people are about to try to kill us."

Chapter
Trillian

I need you to do something for me. Is that all right? Are you willing to do a favor for your favorite author?

Okay, go to your fridge. Dig around inside until you find some lunch meat, cheese, pickles, lettuce, more lunch meat, and some mayonnaise. (And honestly, who chose how to spell that word?* Must be a Librarian ploy to keep me reliant on spellcheck.)

Now, slather some mayo onto two pieces of bread from your pantry. Get it on real good. Are you slathering? I don't think you're slathering. These pages should be mayoized from you trying to read these instructions while

---

* And don't say "the French." Everyone knows they're not real.

you make the food. Now, choose slices of pickle that maximize the outer skin—they're the most crunchy. You can toss the centers. Now, make sure that you salt the cheese.*

You got that? I'll wait. Done? Good. That wasn't so hard, was it?

Now go back in time, teleport to my house in the Free Kingdoms, and give me the sandwich while I'm writing this. I'm kind of hungry.

"Wow," I said softly, staring out *Penguinator*'s cockpit windows.

"You can say that again," Grandpa said. "Mostly because I couldn't hear you the first time. Speak more loudly this time."

"Wow!"

"Much better."

I'd been to Washington, DC, on a school trip once, but it had looked *nothing* like this. *Penguinator* had just come in across Chesapeake Bay, flying right beneath the dense cloud cover. From this high up, I got a good view of the enormous purple dome covering the city in its entirety. It glowed with a violet light, like steam from a hot pan. I lifted off my Oculator's Lenses. Sure enough, without them the dome vanished—save for a warping of the air.

---

* Yes. Salt the cheese.

"That warping?" I asked, pointing.

"Caused by the glass eyes of *Penguinator,*" Kaz said. "Normal people can't see the shield; the glass windows here are designed to give pilots warning of Librarian illusions."

I nodded, lowering my Lenses back on. Kaz and my mother sat at the dashboard—though she was reading nonchalantly—while Grandpa, Draulin, and I had walked up behind their seats to stare out over the landscape. Cousin Dif shoved his way between Grandpa and me, then draped an arm over our shoulders. I saw no sign of his ant farm.

As we drew closer to Washington, I saw a much different city from the one presented to the world. While the outer parts were mostly the same, the center of the downtown—the stuff on all the postcards—was *way* different. The Lincoln Memorial had a turret on top of it, with wicked-looking antiaircraft guns stretching toward the sky, and the long green of the Mall running down from it looked more like a landing strip than a park. The White House had a sharp, red fence rising high around it, and many of the museum buildings had a stretched look to them, rising toward the air, becoming more peaked, more devilish. Only the Washington Monument seemed unchanged: a lone obelisk rising straight into the air, surrounded by darkness.

I easily made out the Highbrary. What appeared in the Hushlands as an innocent, if regal, stone building—the Library of Congress—here manifested as a pitch-black fortress of a structure, stretching six stories high, with wicked stone spires and dark monstrous things flying around it. Say what you will of Librarians, they certainly have style.

I couldn't focus long on the Highbrary, unfortunately, because a fleet of jet planes were scrambling toward us. There had to be a hundred of them, sleek black jets that looked nothing like the planes I'd seen at aircraft museums.

"That must be the entire Librarian Air Force," Kaz said. "Not US military planes—the actual *Librarian* defense force. I've never seen them call out so many before."

"We have them scared," Grandpa said, eager.

"This is incredible!" Dif exclaimed, squeezing my shoulder.

"How silly of me," my mother said, having finally put down her book to join us, "to assume that with you I'd be able to *sneak* into the Highbrary."

"Sneaking is fun," Grandpa said, "but this is *way* more exciting." He paused. "You can dodge them, can't you, Son?"

"Maybe," Kaz said. "I'll need some of you on the outside

though, running defense. Here." He tossed Grandpa a small device that looked like a headset with an earpiece that fit snugly into the ear.

"Communicator's Glass?" Grandpa asked, holding it up.

"Nope. Bluetooth." Kaz handed him a cell phone.

"Librarian technology," Draulin said with a sniff. "Far less advanced than a good shout."

"Yeah, well," Kaz said, tossing me and Draulin a cell phone and headset each, "it works. That's all I care about."

Grandpa was all too eager to put on the headset, though he needed a little help, as he thought the strap that held it in place was an eye patch. (Free Kingdomers often have an . . . unusual perspective on Hushlander technology and customs.) We started up a phone call, all four of us on the line so we could talk easily.

From there, the three of us left Dif, Shasta, and Kaz to make for the exit bay—a room where the wall was retractable. There we equipped ourselves with boots that had Grappler's Glass on the bottom—it would stick to any other kind of glass. I pulled a boot onto my foot.* Doing so gave me a sense of perspective. The last time I'd done

---

* Note.

something like this, I'd been escaping *from* the Hushlands. Now I was heading back, full throttle.

Before, the Librarians had been trying to prevent me from escaping. Now it seemed they would do practically anything they could to keep me out. I was no longer the one being chased. I'd beaten the Librarians in Mokia, and now I was the wolf and they were the sheep. (You know, if sheep had antiaircraft guns, bazookas, and high-tech jet planes.)

This reminds me of hornets.

What? It doesn't remind *you* of hornets? You're pretty strange. I mean this is obviously the *exact* place in a story where you'd expect a discussion of insect biology. It's even listed as such in *The Great Book of How to Write Awesome Books.**

You see, hornets and bees are natural enemies just like cats and dogs, disco and rock, or Bastille's fist and your face. They fought back and forth until one day, the game changed. And that game-changer was the Japanese giant hornet. These monsters managed to get across the ocean (they probably bought a time-share and felt forced to use it) and invade North America.

------

* By Alcatraz Smedry. First edition. It's not published yet though, so the only place you can find it is on my shelf.

This was a problem for the bees. You see, the Japanese giant hornet has tougher skin than any North American hornet. They're more vicious, bigger, and almost impossible for your average honeybee to kill. A few Japanese giant hornets can take out an entire hive—tens of thousands of bees—all by themselves.

So am I the hornet or the bee? Well, it depends on whether Aesop is telling this story or not.

Draulin pulled open the side of *Penguinator,* exposing us to howling wind and a view that twisted my stomach. Grandpa put on a pair of green-tinted spectacles: Windstormer's Lenses, which would let him control the wind and make it easier for us to walk on the outside of the missile-like penguin ship. We filed out, sticking our boots to the floor, then walking out onto a retractable planklike device that extended out the door. From it we could step onto the outside wall of *Penguinator,* relying on our boots to keep us from plummeting to an untimely death on the top of the local Safeway.

Once we were outside, Grandpa pointed. He'd take the central position, above the penguin's head. Draulin— giant crystal sword hefted on her shoulder—marched up to the left side of the ship, and I claimed the right.

Dark clouds rumbled overhead. It might storm soon.

"Welcome to the drive-through," Kaz's voice said over my headset. "May I take your order?"

"Uh . . ." I said back. "What?"

"That's how you start a conversation over radio in the Hushlands," Kaz said. "I've seen it in movies."

"It's not—"

"I'll have a large soda and fries," Grandpa said.

"Do you even know what a large soda is?" I asked him.

"Code phrase," Grandpa replied. "It means 'I acknowledge you, and by the way, please give me some fried potatoes.'"

"I . . . You know what, never mind."

"Anyway," Kaz said over the line, "anyone got any brilliant ideas on how to sneak into the Highbrary?"

"Sneak?" Draulin said. "Might be a little late for that, Lord Smedry."

"Nonsense!" Grandpa said. "We have a rousing battle, then when everyone is exhausted, we slip in."

"Assuming that would somehow work," Draulin said, "how are you planning to bypass the dome?"

"Hmm . . ." Grandpa said.

"How about this," Shasta said loudly over Kaz's line— was she listening in on his conversation? "I think of a plan and you all focus on keeping us from being blown up."

That seemed like a fine idea to me, as the jets were almost upon us. In fact, a pair of them passed by in a scream of engines and a blur of black. I stumbled, then pulled out my Shamefiller's Lens.

Another jet approached, and this one launched a rocket. I yelped, thrusting my Lens forward and sending a jolt of power into it. A wide maroon beam blasted from my hand and struck the missile.

A voice popped into my head.

"Oh, wow. Remember how I jostled the other missiles as I was being loaded? Particularly that cute one? How could I have been so clumsy? And that one time back in the factory? I totally made an inappropriate sound when my casing scraped on the floor. Everyone was looking. Ugh. I wish . . . I wish I could just vanish. . . ."

BOOM.

As the missile vaporized, I lowered the Lens, stunned and more than a little unsettled. From the front of the ship, Grandpa looked back and gave me a thumbs-up. He was still using his Lenses to keep us from getting buffeted by the wind, but enough got through that his wispy hair fluttered around his head.

I felt sick. Had I *guilt-tripped* that missile into self-destructing? It had sounded so pathetic.

It was an inanimate object, I thought. *Why should I care?*

Gritting my teeth, I pointed my Lens as something else shot toward us. The maroon floodlight burst out, and I caught an entire enemy jet in its glow.

"Oh, wow," I heard in my mind—the voice of the plane's pilot. "I can't believe what I said to Jim two years ago. Everyone was having such a good time, and then I bring up his mother. I *knew* she'd died. I'd been at the funeral! But it just slipped out. 'How's your mom?' Why, why did I say that? I could literally explode right—"

I pulled the Lens away, panting, a shock of fear running through me. I felt that if I had waited a moment longer, the pilot *would* have exploded from embarrassment.

Wasn't that the point?

The jet wobbled, then spun out of control, even though my Lens was turned off. I think I saw someone eject. I pretend I did, at least.

Hadn't I always wanted more destructive Lenses? Hadn't I complained about being given "wimpy" Lenses instead? But this . . . this was hitting below the belt. Hearing those voices dredged up all the stupid things *I'd* done in my life, the little mistakes that everyone else has most likely forgotten about. They were the kinds of things you

lie in bed thinking about, feeling foolish. Wishing you could simply vanish.

This was a very, very dangerous Lens. And yet Grandpa considered the other one—the Shaper's Lens—even worse.

What had I gotten myself into?

The penguin dived suddenly; Kaz was taking evasive maneuvers. As we spun through the air, zipping one way and then another, I had to scramble to blow up the odd missile—though I stayed away from attacking the jets.

Fortunately for us, Grandpa and Draulin were far more competent than I was. As she had demonstrated during a previous trip, Draulin had this uncanny ability to jump in front of missiles and bat them away with her sword— like she was playing a very strange game of tennis.* And Grandpa . . .

Well, Grandpa Smedry was a master of Lenses. I found myself distracted, watching him control the wind to blow missiles off course and planes into one another, or nudge *Penguinator* out of the way of a strike. He didn't move; he stood in place, a look of intense concentration on his face, and Lenses *hovered* in front of him. He was using some six

---

* Wouldn't tennis be way more interesting with explosive balls?

or seven at once, sending out blasts of fire, controlling the wind, heightening his awareness of the enemy locations.

He was a ridiculous little man sometimes, but at the same time he was—and I don't use this word lightly here—*astounding.*

He also wasn't going to be enough. Our ship was better than the Librarian ones, our pilot was amazing, and my grandfather was fighting wonderfully—but we were barely staying ahead of the missiles and the machine guns and the gun emplacements. Kaz couldn't keep us on a straight course; he had to twist us to the sides to avoid barrages.

After ten minutes of furious battle, we were no closer to breaking through than we had been.

"I can't help thinking," Draulin said as she sliced a missile in half, "that this assault wasn't very well-thought-out."

"How surprising," my mother's voice said in our ears.

"Do you have a plan for us?" I asked her, then spun toward a missile and focused my Lens on it. The poor thing thought about how its serial numbers were misprinted and blew up. Bits of shrapnel bounced off *Penguinator* around me.

"Yes," Shasta said. "But it requires us to *not* be the center of attention for a few moments."

"So, basically impossible," I said. "I mean, we *are* Smedrys."

"I hadn't noticed," Shasta said. "For once it would be nice if you people didn't hog all the attention."

"My dear," Grandfather said over the line, panting, sounding exhausted, "you must not have been paying attention. You see, this is what Smedrys do best."

"Smell funny?" Kaz asked.

"Make my life difficult?" Draulin asked.

"Eat your chips when your back is turned?" I asked.

"No," Grandpa said. "Draw fire."

All was still for a moment.

"Pine nuts!" Kaz cursed. "Someone is calling us on the ship's Communicator's Glass."

"Answer, and tell them you'll hold the phone up to the glass, please," Grandpa said.

Kaz did so, and an unfamiliar voice crackled in over the line. "Welcome to the drive-through. May I take your order please?"

"Large soda and whatnot," I said back. "Who is this?"

"Lord Smedry! We saw your call to arms. It appeared in every window!"

"Uh, that's great," I said. Shattering Glass. How far *had* my little display gone? "But who *are* you?"

Shadows appeared in the clouds above us, and then at

least *fifty* glass ships of a variety of shapes descended through them. "Unified Free Kingdoms Air Guard," the voice said. "We had been dispatched to help clean up Tuki Tuki, but . . . well, we couldn't do much there. So we figured we might as well see if you needed some air support. Unless you'd rather destroy them all on your own, my lord."

"No, no," I said. "I'm quite willing to share the destroying. This time. A guy needs to learn to share."

"Very good, my lord."

And with that, the *real* fighting began.

° Deckard °

A h, the wooly sea sloth, with its luscious fur and its body made of high-grade aluminum. It is a noble creature, and endangered; as of this writing there are precisely negative four of them remaining in the wild—as opposed to a hundred years ago, when there were none of them living off the coast of Newfoundland.

The wooly sea sloth is known for a steady diet of conservative talk show hosts and Twix bars with all the chocolate licked off. The peaceful animal is of no danger to anyone, since none of them exist or have ever existed, and yet their habitat is threatened by their only natural predator: Wikipedia.

Stop Wikipedia rampages now and support the wooly sea sloth reforestation project, led by six former presidents of the United States (one a zombie) and no conservative talk show hosts.*

"You knew those ships were coming," I said, scrambling up to my grandfather, still on the top of *Penguinator.*

"I hoped," he replied, taking down the Lenses that had been hovering in front of him, then tucking them away. "When the monarchs said they'd sent the air guard, and when your speech got broadcast through the whole city . . . well, I figured those soldiers would feel bad for having abandoned Mokia."

"They're disobeying orders," Draulin said, clomping up to us.

"Thank goodness!" Grandpa said.

Draulin gave him a glare that could have bathed a hippopotamus.

"It's not a *total* infraction, Draulin," Grandpa said. "The monarchs sent the air guard to 'help you Smedrys.' Technically, my grandson outranks most people in the Free Kingdoms. Without a countermand, his invitation

---

* This section was included in the book so that when a Librarian walks past, you can quickly flip to this page. When they read over your shoulder—as they always do, because they're annoying—you will appear to be reading a science book about the noble wooly sea sloth. I've therefore saved your life, and so you really should be getting around to making me that sandwich.

to join him in an assault was practically an executive order!"

"It's not right. They're not following *protocol*."

"Can you just please be happy we're not dead?" I said. "This once. I promise you we can die next time."

"Fine," she grumbled. "As long as we do it by the book."

"What book?" Grandpa asked as we crossed the back of *Penguinator*.

She hesitated. "You know, I'm not actually sure."

"I'll write one someday," I said. "Then you can follow what I say to do in that one."

"Oh. Joy."

My grandfather climbed back into the vehicle first, Draulin following. I lingered on the roof.

Around me, missiles detonated. Jets whizzed past. Explosions, smoke, fire. Down below, innocent suburbs smoldered as the Librarian forces clashed with the Free Kingdomer flying machines. The sound was like fireworks popping all around me, and we flew through a wave of smoke pouring from a dying ship as it spiraled downward.

I had caused this. I had brought them. I *was* happy to not have to fight the Librarians on my own, but in that moment all of it was hard for me to take in. A lot of people were going to get hurt by this, and many of them wouldn't deserve it.

I'd berated the monarchs for their unwillingness to commit to war, yet when I'd had the chance to bring down Librarian jet fighters, I'd pulled back, frightened of the damage I might do.

I was the worst kind of coward. The kind who would let others die, so long as he didn't have to be involved.

I tromped down below, letting Grandpa close the door. The two of us made our way to the cockpit, though I left the Grappler's Glass boots on. Kaz was doing a lot of swerving, and without the boots I'd have been thrown against the wall repeatedly.

In the cockpit, Cousin Dif gave a whoop of excitement. "That was amazing! You two are just the best. Nothing says 'Smedry' like a last-minute rescue!"

"Yes indeed," Grandpa said.

"I mean, you *could* have warned us," Dif said, "letting us prepare better and not making us feel like we were all going to die. But instead you left us in the dark so there could be a dramatic reveal! It was perfect."

"Yeah," Grandpa said, deflating. "I suppose. Heh. Well."

Dif continued, "Someone else would have figured that in not telling everyone the dramatic plan, we might have accidentally done something to ruin it—like Kaz dodging up into the sky above the clouds and leading the Librarian ships directly to the unprepared Free Kingdom vessels, but *you* know that the true Smedry way is—"

"Ahem," Grandfather said. "Shasta? You mentioned a plan?"

"Yes," she said, rotating in her seat. "We need to get down there without the Librarians knowing we've landed. So, we have Kaz make a run at a Librarian antiaircraft turret, then swerve into the streets as it fires. In the smoke the blasts produce, he can drop us to the ground."

We waited for more.

"Uh," I said, "that's it?"

"I didn't have a lot of time to think," she said with a huff. "But there *is* a little more. We record your grandfather saying some idiotically characteristic things, then play them at wide distribution. The Librarians will intercept our channels and think he's still on the ship, so they won't hunt for us as we're breaking in."

"Huh," Kaz said. "So we use the attempt to break in as a cover for us attempting to break in?"

"Something like that."

"I like it!" Grandpa said, pointing toward the air.

"Blast," Shasta said. "You're supposed to think it's too boring."

"What's boring?" Grandpa said. "After all, we'll need to hurl ourselves from a full-speed penguin!"

"Moving?" Shasta said. "I was thinking we'd land."

"No time for that," Grandpa said. "This is going to be fun! Kazan, let's record some video of me taunting the Librarians. Then we'll jump out!"

"Sure thing, Pop," Kaz said. "But you realize I'll have to stay behind and fly the ship."

"Oh," Grandpa said. "Couldn't Dif—"

"Can't fly!" Dif said happily. "And didn't you want me along to give commentary on Hushlander culture?"

"I suppose I did." Grandpa took a deep breath. "It is what must be. You'll be our escape plan, Son."

Kaz nodded.

"It's settled then!" Dif said. "I'm going to go pack."

"Pack?" I asked. "What is there to pack? We just picked you up."

"I need to find some crazy things to bring along!" Dif said. "A sock or two, some string, a bug, anything *wacky* and *crazy* that nobody will expect! Then we can use them to save the day unexpectedly! Right guys? Huh?"

He scuttled from the room.

"I *really* hate that guy," Kaz said under his breath.

"Kaz!" Grandpa said. "He's merely trying to fit in."

"I think he's making fun of us," Kaz said.

I shook my head. I didn't think it was that; he was too earnest. He *did* want to be like the other Smedrys. But

when he pointed things out as he did . . . well, that just
made them sound dumb. Like how being forced to explain
a joke ruins it.

As my grandfather went to his room to use the Communicator's Glass there to record some properly Smedryesque
messages, I stepped between Kaz and my mother, looking
out the windshield eyes. We dodged through the middle of
a battle, moving so quickly that it was hard to track what
was happening. Kaz dived, and my stomach lurched. To
the left, a giant glass bat had grabbed a jet plane in its
feet. To the right, a horned owl had a gaping, jagged hole
in one of its sides.

"We'll need to do something about that dome," Shasta
said. "How do we get through?"

I reached into my pocket and fingered the Shamefiller's
Lens. "Can you open these windows for me?"

"Sure," Kaz said. "Might get a little windy in here
though."

"Let's try it."

Kaz nodded, dodging us out of the way of a firing gun
emplacement, then hit a button on the glass dashboard.
One of the penguin's eye-windows retracted.

My ears popped and a rush of wind hit me in the face.
It's shocking how hard it is to breathe with so much air
coming so quickly. It's like trying to eat popcorn fired at

you by a bazooka. Still, I was able to raise the Shamefiller's Lens and point it at the dome. My hair whipping about on my head, my bow tie fluttering, I focused a blast of energy into the Lens and let loose a concentrated beam of humiliation at the dome.

"I can't believe I stopped those three Librarians at the perimeter," said a loud, deep voice in my head, "all because they were carrying confiscated bits of glass. The entire army went on alert, and everyone thought they were double agents! I could have just crumbled upon myself with shame. I should have seen, shouldn't have stopped them."

I waited, listening, but nothing was happening.

"The dome's too strong!" Kaz said. "Should I turn us away? We're heading straight for it!"

"Hold steady!" I said, driving more power into the Lens. It started to get warm in my fingers.

"And the shame of not being able to keep the rain off people! I'm a dome. I should be able to keep things dry. At least provide shade? But nobody can even see me! All I do is scan for glass Lenses that almost never come this way. What good am I really? Then there was the moment with the Scrivener. . . ."

What?

"Alcatraz?" Kaz said, urgent.

"Keep going!" I shouted, pumping more energy. The Lens was getting hot, like the glass I'd melted earlier. That seemed very dangerous.

"I stopped him, of all people," the dome's voice said, "just because he had a Lens on him. Everyone saw it. I can't believe—"

The Lens burned my fingers. I cried out as a section of the dome exploded, opening a hole the size of a large building.

I dropped the Lens, wagging my fingers. I'd burned them good, but the Lens—fortunately—hadn't melted. It hit the floor with a plink and rolled to the side. Kaz let out a whoop and steered us right through the hole, then pushed a button to close the window. Many of the other Free Kingdomer ships followed us through immediately.

I sucked on my fingers.

"Nice work," Kaz said.

I nodded absently. The dome had mentioned the Scrivener. I could only assume that an inanimate object wasn't going to lie in its own thoughts.* Someone really was calling himself the Scrivener. An ominous title.

"Hey, what's that column of smoke?" I said.

---

* I don't know why I made the assumption that inanimate objects don't lie. This book has lied to you several times already.

Kaz followed my gesture. Near the center of DC—not a great distance from the towering Washington Monument and the Mall—a line of smoke rose between some of the buildings.

"A crash perhaps?" Kaz said. "Or a stray missile?"

"Could be," Shasta replied, "but the dome would have stopped most missiles and a lot of debris."

"I think someone else is fighting back," I said. "That smoke is from three or four different buildings, all burning. And . . . is that a barricade?"

We were past too quickly to make out more.

"You guys should go get ready for the drop," Kaz said, steering us over the center of DC.

"Try to keep it level, if you can," Shasta said.

"Tall order," Kaz said. "And I, by definition, am not particularly good at those. I'll see what I can do."

Shasta rose to leave, but Kaz reached out and took her by the arm. "What are you going to do when you find him?" he asked her. "Have you thought about that?"

"Of course I have," she said. "I'm going to stop him."

"Will you kill him?" Kaz asked, meeting her eyes.

"I love him, Kaz," my mother said.

"That doesn't answer my question."

She pulled her arm away. "I'll do what I have to. If that means pulling the trigger, then so be it."

She stalked away. I recovered my Shamefiller's Lens, which had cooled enough to handle, and followed. Their conversation left me feeling a little out of place in my own story, which should never happen. So let's talk some more about me.

Alcatraz was a silly Oculator boy who had a proclivity for stopping a story at a stoopid point to start an additional story. On occasion, Alcatraz put words such as "cockapoo" into his books. That word in particular brought him vast humiliation on two occasions. Sadly, his boss didn't spot said words, for both cockapoos hid in a long paragraph about Alcatraz's most amazing points—and rational folk usually skip such things. Alcatraz is guilty of casually ripping apart causality to find a sandwich, is guilty of occasionally imitating a fish, and is guilty of hating baby cats. Also, writing full paragraphs without any *E*s is hard.

"Would you really kill him?" I asked my mother, catching up to her in the glass hallway.

"Yes. And you? If the fate of the world hinged on your answer, could you kill your father, Alcatraz?"

"I . . ." I swallowed.

"You'd better be able to," she said. "I spent your entire life trying to make a hard man out of you. If the time comes, child, you stop him. Whatever it takes."

Such a cold response. I didn't want to think about what

she'd said. There would be another way to stop my father. We could talk some sense into him. Right?

Shasta didn't seem to think so. She'd always been like that—so knowing, so certain, so *smug*. She didn't so much as stumble as Kaz swerved *Penguinator*; she merely leaned against the wall with one hand and remained in place.

It made me want to do something to disturb her calm.

"Is the Scrivener really still alive?" I asked.

Shasta spun on me. "Where did you hear that?"

"I reversed one of the Librarian bugs we found," I said. "We overheard She Who Cannot Be Named talking about the Scrivener. Biblioden. He can't possibly still be alive."

Shasta studied me. "There are . . . rumors. I never gave them much credence, but recently talk has grown. Some claim to have spoken with him, to have been given orders by him. If Kangchenjunga has joined the believers . . . well, she's not one to be easily taken in. Either she's playing along for some reason, or something convinced her."

Shasta seemed troubled. That was a welcome departure from smugness, but I hadn't provoked the reaction I'd wanted. I considered doing something *really* upsetting, like telling her I'd decided to write fantasy novels for a living, but there was no call to be so extreme. Even I need to have *some* standards.

We again reached the room with the exit bay, and I pulled off my Grappler's Glass boots and stowed them. Beneath, through the glass floor, I could see the city passing in a blur. We were lower than before, but still *way* too high to survive a jump. "So . . . um," I said to my mother, "how do you think we're going to—"

Cousin Dif burst into the room, wearing a backpack and bunny slippers. They were an odd match to his plaid shirt and bow tie, and he'd swapped his pants for a pair of very pink shorts.

"Hushlander disguise in place!" he proclaimed.

"I thought they said you'd lived over here," I said.

"I have! I did an extended internship in San Francisco."

"What sort of internship?" I asked, skeptical.

"On a wilderness preserve," Dif said. "With tents, and animal trainers, and lots of people in bleachers."

"A . . . circus?"

"Yes! That's what it was called. I worked among them for years, observing how to dress and act around Hushlanders until my skills for infiltration were perfected." He paused. "Oh, I almost forgot! No wonder you're skeptical." He reached into his backpack and took out a top hat and put it on his head. "There. Perfect Hushlander costume!"

I was speechless. Sometimes being confronted by monumental stupidity does that to me.* Before I could recover, Draulin joined us.

She wore a sleek blue evening gown with sequins and a slit up the side, her hair done up as if for prom, her lips bright red. Long gloves covered her arms almost all the way up to her shoulders.

My eyes bulged almost out of my skull.

Draulin was a *woman*?

Okay, so maybe I'm not one to be making wisecracks about other people's monumental stupidity. I mean, I knew that Draulin was Bastille's mother, wife of the king

---

* That might explain why I never said anything that time I visited your house.

of Nalhalla. But . . . you know, I'd kind of always imagined that she slept in her armor.

"Great costume," Dif said.

"Thank you, Lord D'if," Draulin said, fiddling in her handbag—which, if it was like Bastille's, held her sword in a mildly impossible pocket of space-time. "Lord Kazan, is your line still open?"

"Yup."

"Will these Hushlander transmission devices work inside the Highbrary?"

"They should."

"Excellent. We will be in touch. Be careful up here, Lord Kazan. Do not forget you carry my daughter in this ship."

"I'll try not to get us blown up," Kaz said.

It took a few more minutes—as one might expect—before my grandfather decided to join us. Being late wasn't only his Smedry Talent, it was a way of life. He finally trotted in, carrying a roll of cloth, and grinned at Draulin. "It really is just like old times!"

"Are you going to sink this city too?" Draulin asked him.

"That happened *one* time," Grandpa said. "And everyone got out. Mostly." He began distributing pieces of cloth.

I took mine with a frown. It was about the size of a towel, and was thin and white. What was this?

Grandpa pulled open the wide bay door on the side of *Penguinator*. Wind whipped at us, loud enough that I could barely hear Kaz say, "I'll steer us through that smoke Alcatraz spotted earlier. That would be a great place to jump, as you'll be hidden from anyone watching."

"Yes," I began, "but—"

"A great place to jump?" Dif said. "Out we go then!"

And he shoved me right out the door.

Chapter

Frog

You may have noticed the odd numbering of chapters in this book. Then again, maybe you haven't noticed. I mean, we both know you aren't exactly the sharpest sword in the armory. If you *were* the smart type, you'd be doing something more productive with your time than reading this book. Like, say, swimming with hungry alligators or eating thumbtacks.

We'll pretend for now that you noticed the chapter names. Good for you. Here, have a cookie.

No, it's not a dog biscuit. Why would you think I'd try to give you a dog biscuit? Simply because they were on sale.

As I plummeted to my death, I at least got to check

off "Jump out of a giant flying glass penguin without a parachute" from my list of things to accomplish in life.*

Granted, I didn't want to check "die" off my list just yet. This left me in a difficult spot. And then another. And then another. (You see, I kept moving and leaving one spot for the next, as will happen when you're plummeting at high velocity through the air.)

Fortunately, I had barely enough time to wrap myself in the towel-like length of cloth Grandpa had given me. Then I crashed into the ground.

And bounced.

You see, glassweave cloth can be very helpful for not dying. It had saved Bastille on numerous occasions, and this time it saved me. I was left with a very broken sheet of cloth—cracked like glass—but I survived. Dif plowed into the ground beside me, then Grandpa, my mother, and finally Draulin. We're Smedrys (well, most of us), and so diving face-first into danger is both our primary method of attack *and* our backup plan.

Overhead, *Penguinator* blasted away, and a few Librarian jets chased after it. I hoped the pilots hadn't seen us make the drop-off, though that hope was a flimsy one.

---

* What, it's not on your bucket list?

We'd gone too early because of Dif's interference; the line of smoke I'd seen earlier was still several streets off.

"Well, that was fun," Grandpa said as he climbed to his feet. "Anyone dead?"

"Does my pride count?" Draulin asked, dusting herself off.

"I don't think so," Grandpa said. "I killed that years ago. Dif, I appreciate your enthusiasm, but shoving my grandson out of planes is usually my job. So next time, kindly refrain until I give the word."

"Sorry, sir," Dif said, looking abashed.

"Now then," Grandpa said, "suggestions on what to do next?"

"Run?" Shasta asked.

"Well, I don't really need the exercise right now, as—"

The building beside us exploded. Troops wearing bow ties and sweater vests barreled around a corner farther down the street, carrying guns.

"Ah," Grandpa said. "So our hasty drop was spotted, was it? That's disappointing. I think—"

"Run!" I said, towing him after me as we all scrambled around a corner. Several of the Librarians started firing, but we managed to get out of their line of sight.

"This way to the Highbrary," Shasta said, turning down a street.

"No," I said, turning the opposite direction. "This way."
I barreled forward, and fortunately the others joined me,
though Shasta complained vociferously.

I ran us through a little garden between two large
buildings with ancient-looking stonework. The streets
here were wide, yet desolate. I didn't see a soul—other
than the Librarians chasing us—until I stumbled upon a
group of terrified people huddled in a small touristy shop.

It was a shock to see people in normal clothing. A clash
between my old life and my new one. I was actually back
in the Hushlands. America. Nearby a cracked doorway
looked in on a convenience store, where a television on the
counter was playing to a group of worried people. I slowed
here.

Inside, the television displayed a reporter holding a
stack of papers, with a blurry picture of the DC area on
the screen beside him. ". . . Nobody knows the nature of
the invaders, though some eyewitnesses claim to have
seen strange, baffling technology. . . ."

I started running again as Draulin passed, hauling me
after her. Shattering Glass . . . how must all this look to
the common people? A crazy assault out of nowhere? A
defending army nobody recognized? The Librarians ruled
in secret.

Or they had. Cleaning all of this up would take a *whole*

lot of memory toads. That brought a smile to my lips—
one that was quite nearly ripped clean off as a Librarian
mortar exploded on the street.

I was thrown to the ground, but as a hail of bullets came
from our pursuers, I found Draulin standing crouched
between me and the Librarians, arm raised before her face,
her glassweave dress and gloves blocking the fire.

Funny thing about Knights of Crystallia—they complain *all the time* about us Smedrys getting into danger, yet
they seem attracted to danger like a novelist to bad puns.*

"Go!" Draulin ordered.

I went.

"This sure is exciting!" Cousin Dif said, glancing over
his shoulder as I ran past him to lead the way again. He
seemed completely unrepentant, considering that we'd
only been spotted because he'd forced us to jump early.

"Where are we going?" Shasta demanded as we lurched
around a corner, passing an abandoned cart full of T-shirts
and miniature flags.

I pointed ahead, hoping that my gut instinct was right.
I had seen something down here, hadn't I? Someone fighting back? Because if I was wrong, we were likely dead.

---

* Indeed, she seemed to be able to spot danger far more easily than I
could. I guess she had knight vision.

But no . . . that *was* a barricade, formed out of wooden furniture—most of it desks with lots of little drawers. People hid behind the sides and top of the barricade, though I couldn't make out any details.

It didn't matter. If they were fighting, then they were on our side. I led the others toward the barricade, Librarians on our tail. Just a little farther and . . .

One of the people on the barricade stood up. He wore a bow tie, a sweater vest, and horn-rimmed glasses.

A Librarian.

I stumbled to a halt.

A *Librarian.*

Whoever had been fighting back—if indeed anyone ever had been—the Librarians had already gotten to them. That meant I'd put my family directly between two enemy forces. No place to run—the road dead-ended at the barricade, with buildings burning to either side.

Everyone pulled to a stop around me, Grandpa with Lenses out, Draulin clutching her sword—her swanky evening gown riddled with cracked bullet marks.

The Librarians behind us had nearly caught up.

"Now," Grandpa said, his voice tense, "would be an *excellent* time for the Talents to return, don't you think, Alcatraz? Very dramatic."

"I don't . . . I don't know how. . . ."

"Try," Grandpa said. "You are the focus of the blood-line, lad. You have the Talent in its most pure form. That's why you were able to break it."

"I don't fix things, Grandpa," I whispered. "I only break them."

"Try," he repeated.

I didn't even know where to start. Unbreak the Talents? Grandpa might as well have told me to breathe under-water, count from one to a sasquatch, or write a book without making fun of anyone. How *did* I manipulate the Talents?

I tried flexing, then thinking really hard. Nothing hap-pened of course, though I did think for a moment that I saw something. Reflected in the glass of a broken window nearby—a storefront. That window reflected a version of me, except wrong. A translucent, shadowy version of me.

The Bane of Incarna, they had written in the tomb of Alcatraz the First. *That which twists, that which corrupts, and that which destroys.*

The Dark Talent.

I stared at that off reflection for far too long, and I thought I saw something deeper behind it. A city? With ancient architecture, columns and marble? Burning?

The Librarians behind us pulled up into the street and leveled guns at us. We were dead.

The Librarians on the barricade suddenly started *shooting* at the ones who had been chasing us.

In the storm of gunfire that followed, a bullet struck the remaining storefront glass and shattered it. I was shocked back into the moment—which is rather a pity, since if I'd gotten shot right then the book could have ended. That means I could have stopped writing and gone to get a pizza! Instead, by not getting killed, my past self forced me to keep on working today. What a jerk.

Grandpa pulled me along toward the barricade, and only then did I see a familiar figure standing atop it—a woman with dark skin, wearing a leather skirt studded with spikes, a white bodice, and a long cloak embroidered with little open books. She wore horn-rimmed glasses that had a chain on them, and was packing an enormous machine gun with an attached grenade launcher.

Himalaya Smedry, good Librarian.

Her husband, my cousin Folsom, helped us scramble over the barricade. He was a lanky, dark-haired man whose Smedry Talent was (had been?) dancing really, really badly.

Himalaya and some others laid down suppressive fire.*

---

* That's a fancy term for shooting like crazy and hoping your enemy gets scared and hides instead of shooting back.

I put my back to the barricade, out of danger, as Draulin came over the top, last in line. Incredibly, our entire team seemed safe. Or at least as safe as one could feel while surrounded by Librarians.

It was hard to differentiate this group from the one that had chased us. Similar clothing, similarly armed with a variety of Hushlander weaponry. The only difference was the symbol of the open book; some wore it on an armband, others on a headband.

"Not that I'm complaining about the timely rescue," Grandpa said, "but who exactly are you folks?"

"Librarian Liberation Libationists!" one of them shouted.

". . . Libationists?" I asked.

"It's alliterative!" Folsom exclaimed.

"But that doesn't have anything to do with . . . You know what, never mind." I gave Folsom a hug. "It's good to see you two. Seems you've been busy." Last I'd seen them, they'd been determined to go to the Hushlands and distribute pamphlets to Librarians on not being evil.

It appeared they'd gone a little beyond pamphlets.

"We couldn't leave you to fight this battle on your own!" Himalaya said, climbing down the barricade and setting her gun on her shoulder. "Though honestly, we worried you wouldn't show up. You took your sweet time getting here."

"I told you, dear," Folsom said. "Lord Leavenworth was with them. They're always going to be late."

"Then we should have delayed and come later ourselves."

"They'd still have been late."

"But—"

He patted her on the shoulder. Himalaya was a Smedry by marriage, and had a Talent because of the union—but she was still a Librarian. She wanted things to make sense. I couldn't blame her for that.

"But how did you know I was coming to Washington, DC?" I asked. "Do you have some spies in the Free Kingdoms?"

"Spies?" Folsom asked. "Alcatraz, you appeared on our window."

I blinked. "I *did*?"

"Sure," Himalaya said. "Your face was on every piece of glass in the country—both magical and mundane."

Grandpa sniffed; he didn't like calling silimatic glass magical. It was a common source of disagreement between Free Kingdomers and Hushlanders. I didn't care much about that; I was simply stunned.

How had my declaration traveled this far? Every piece of glass in the *country*?

No wonder the Librarians were frightened. How were

they going to cover *this* up? And where had I gotten such power? I'd never done anything on this level before.

"We're ready to fight," said one of the other Librarians. "We've been through a six-hundred-fifteen-step program. We're totally not evil anymore."

"Except Frank," another Librarian noted, pointing toward a buff Librarian with glasses wrapped in tape and two massive swords strapped to his back. "He's still a little evil."

"I like to eat all of the red and green gummy bears out of a bag," Frank said with a thick German accent. "And leave the orange ones behind."

"You monster," I said, aghast.

"It is a compulsion," Frank said. "Don't judge me."

The gunfire stopped, which was a welcome reprieve. The Librarians who had been fighting atop the barricade climbed down. "They retreated," one said, "but with Smedrys in here, they're bound to come back—or just shell our position."

"We can't stay then," Himalaya said. "Lord Smedry, what is your plan?"

I glanced toward my grandfather.

"This is your infiltration, lad," he said to me. "You're in charge."

"We need to get into the Highbrary," I said, "and stop

my father from reaching the secret Forgotten Language archives inside."

"That's going to stop the Bibliodenites?" Himalaya asked. "And save the world?"

"Uh . . ." I said, glancing at Shasta and my grandfather. "Will it?"

"Who knows!" Grandpa said. "But letting a whole pack of Smedrys free in the middle of the biggest Librarian stronghold on earth can't be particularly *good* for their organization, wouldn't you say?"

Himalaya and Folsom looked at each other, then both shrugged. "Good enough for me," Himalaya said. "I've got about a hundred troops loaded with weapons and pamphlets."

"Pamphlets?" I asked. "Isn't it a little late for that?"

"Nah," Folsom said. "They're *Librarians*. They basically have to read anything you throw at them."

"It is a compulsion," the German Librarian said. "Don't judge us."

"They may not believe what the pamphlets say," Folsom said, "but the tactic works as a distraction sometimes." He grinned. "I like wrapping them around grenades."

"My force," Himalaya said, "will make an assault and break into the Highbrary. You can slip in during the fighting."

"Covering up our breaking in by breaking in?" Draulin asked. "That worked *so* well last time."

"It's the best chance we have," I said. "We'll do it, Himalaya. But how are you going to break into the place?"

"Well," Himalaya said, "I've been in the Highbrary before, and it's bigger than people think. It's built into caverns that stretch beneath the entire downtown." She pointed her gun at the ground. "So if you want to get in, you basically just have to go down."

"That's great," Shasta said, "and impossible. The caverns will be shielded. We can't exactly *dig* and find our way in, now can we? How do you propose we make an opening?"

"I figure," Himalaya said, glancing at Folsom, "we could simply use the Smedrys to do what they do best."

"Draw fire?" I asked.

"Draw fire?" Grandpa asked.

"Draw fire?" Dif asked.*

"How did you guess?" Himalaya said with a grin. "Go stand out in the open over there, if you please...."

---

* Also, draw fire.

Chapter

Alice

I consider it my duty to enlighten and educate you, my readers, about life and its mysteries. I figure this is particularly important for my readers in the Hushlands, who suffer under Librarian oppression. Often they don't even know what they don't know!*

Sometimes what I teach you has to do with technology, the Free Kingdoms, and Librarian secrets. But sometimes it's important to give you general life lessons. I'm certain you appreciate all the thought, work, and research I do in order to bring you the most significant, informative, and *important* lessons that I can.

People are disgusting.

---

* They must not read enough footnotes.

No, really. We're pretty gross. We're always sniffling, coughing, shuffling, burping, slurping, and, uh, making other noises. We do so much of this that in order not to explode from the embarrassment of it all, we have gotten pretty good at ignoring these nonverbal sounds. You want some proof? Try this totally scientific and very meaningful experiment. Sneak up on someone* who is awake, but doing something quiet, like reading a book or assembling a doomsday bomb.

Then write down every strange noise they make. Go ahead. Make a list, then give it to them once they notice you. I guarantee they'll be totally appreciative of your opening their ears to all of the strange sounds they emit.

They may even make a few new noises when reading the list.

Dif, Grandpa, and I wandered out into the middle of the open street a safe distance away from the barricade.

I let out a strangled sound.

Dif yipped in excitement and began running in circles. Following Himalaya's orders, I reluctantly began jumping up and down and waving my arms.

Grandpa grunted, looking upward. Above, a group of

---

* Siblings are preferable.

Librarian jets crossed the sky, and I had little doubt that they'd spotted us.

From the barricade, Himalaya gave us a thumbs-up.

I'll admit that I had a moment of doubt here. Perhaps it was my cowardly nature asserting itself. Or instead perhaps it was the thought of being blown up, which is a method of dying that's on my list of ways to die that don't sound very fun.*

---

* Also on that list: decapitation, drowning, falling to my death, being shot, being stabbed, being eaten by a wildebeest, being eaten by a tamebeest, being eaten by anything else, heart attacks, cancer, death by gratuitous paper cuts, burning to death, golf-ball-inna-face-itis, falling into the sun, catching malaria, being forced to watch too many Korean soap operas, getting in a car wreck, being hit by a bus, dysentery, tuberculosis, consumption (in case they're different), having a piano fall on me, being forced to go back in time and accidentally killing my own great-great-grandfather in a clichéd science fiction action sequence, getting mauled by a feral T. rex, snakebite, SADS (Sudden Alcatraz Death Syndrome), the plague, choking, spontaneous combustion, zombies, getting trampled by an elephant, eating rocks, being eaten by rocs, being punched by The Rock, Mongol invasion, alien invasion, kitten invasion, poisoning, balefire, arrow to the knee, being drawn and quartered, hanging, crucifixion, being fed to lions, anything else the Romans did to people, eating too many breath mints, wandering into "da hood" wearing an ill-designed Karl's Kind Kinesiology T-shirt, being shanked, elevator malfunction, heat death of the universe, almonds, electrocution, suffocation, running with scissors, accidental grenade ingestion, being sucked up a tornado, *Avada*

For a second, I doubted Himalaya. What if she really *was* an evil Librarian? What if this was her way of dealing with us Smedrys once and for all?

The planes roared overhead, coming back around.

I let out a whimper.

Bombs dropped. And these weren't your ordinary bombs either. Covered in spikes, painted a pure black, if I'd been looking closely instead of panicking I'd have seen that they had SMEDRYBUSTER 2300 stenciled on them. Himalaya had explained that she'd seen them—weapons designed specifically to deal with members of my family— hanging under the wings of ships above. They'd deliver a concentrated explosion at the point of impact, creating a column of lava that would rise a hundred feet in the air and burrow an equal amount down.

You see, by this point the Librarians had learned that there was no such thing as overkill when it came to dealing with my family. Much like how after discovering an

---

Kedavra, being sued by J. K. Rowling, bee sting, Sting beating, lightning strike, radiation poisoning, stroke, accidental teddy bear detonation, being eaten by a sentient romance novel, quicksand, explosive diarrhea, really *any* kind of diarrhea, parasites, diabetes, hypertension, rocket-powered turbo slugs, eating paint, concrete shoes, death by ants, death by aunts, measles, starvation, dehydration, circus accident, and accidentally putting something metal in the microwave.

infestation of kittens in your basement you might as well burn down your entire house, the Librarians consider it worth a little collateral damage* to kill a Smedry.

This was, of course, exactly what we wanted. Those bombs would open up a nice tunnel that would burrow into the Highbrary. There was only one problem—the little fact that we were between the bombs and the ground.

————

* i.e. "Accidentally burning a hole through the center of our city."

I yelped as the bombs whooshed toward us, and Himalaya's Librarians cheered. Cousin Dif blew his nose. (I realize this isn't really relevant, but you notice all kinds of new things in a chapter without proper dialogue.) I scrambled away, feet grinding on asphalt, wondering just how we were supposed to get out of this.

Ahead, Himalaya gestured to us urgently. Was that "Talents" she was mouthing?

She didn't realize the Talents didn't work.

That . . . was going to be a problem.

As we scrambled away, my grandfather whooped and whipped out the Windstormer's Lenses he'd been using to control the wind up above. He grinned, then pointed the Lenses directly at the ground beneath us.

The Lenses let out a burst of wind. A really, *really* strong burst of wind—as he'd mentioned, I wasn't the only one whose ability with Lenses was undergoing a strange enhancement. The wind roared, rushing and flipping us all away, scattered like leaves.

The bombs hit.

"Gak!" went Alcatraz.

"BOOOM!" went the bombs.

"Snore," went Bastille.

"Whee!" went Grandpa.

"Groan," went my mother.

"Caporch,"* went the ground.

"Moo," goes the cow.

"Yaaaaaaa!" went Dif.

"Gak!" went Alcatraz again.

"Roar!" went the wind.

"Thunk," went my head as I slammed into a building. I made a quite unique moaning sound as I collapsed to the ground.

A short time later, Draulin nudged me with the tip of her boot. "Hmmm?" she asked.

"Bleh," I said, feeling nauseous. Grandpa's blast of wind had thrown me to safety, but it hadn't felt pleasant. I groaned as I stumbled to my feet.

In front of me, the street had been reduced to a large, smoldering hole. Burned sections of ground crackled softly. As I watched, Himalaya's freedom fighters dug out from under the debris or appeared from behind bits of rubble, many looking dazed. They saw the open hole and let out a series of battle cries, then pulled out pamphlets in one hand and machine guns in the other before charging toward the pit.

My team, looking a little the worse for wear, gathered

---

* The sound of concrete ripping up in a bomb's explosion, obviously.

on the lip of the pit. Everyone looked alive, although with Draulin you can never tell for sure—at any moment, I figured she might turn out to be a log that's really good at faking.

I gestured to the hole. "Mmm?"

"Mmm!" Dif said, chewing on a candy bar he'd found in the rubble.

Himalaya's team set out ropes and began rappelling down into the hole. I leaned out, looking into the blackness. It was *deep*. I thought I saw little fires down below. The remnants of the explosion?

I took a breath, then grabbed one of the ropes—a knotted one they'd placed for me—and began to climb down into the Highbrary.

Chapter

° Marco °

I feel the need to post a warning here.

I've played a lot of tricks on you, my dear reader, during the production of these five volumes of my autobiography. I've been deceptive, manipulative, and even malicious. This was all in the name of the greater good: proving to you (rather than simply telling you) the sort of person I am.

The end is here. This time I'm not being silly. This time I'm not lying. You won't get to the end of this volume and find me saying, "Ha, just kidding!" This is indeed the end.

And I fail.

I know what's going through your head right now. You're expecting some kind of twist or redemption. You're thinking, *Oh, Alcatraz. You've fooled me too many times so* *far! I'm not falling for this one. I* know *you actually win in the end.**

I've worked hard to train you into this attitude. You see, I've understood from the beginning that the best way to trick you is to be honest. That's the last thing you'd expect from me.

I want you to feel like I do, to know the hurt I know.

This is the only way.

I clung to the rope, climbing down into the pit. Falling a hundred feet into a smoking hole in the middle of Washington, DC, wasn't currently on my list of unfun ways to die, but I quickly added it just in case. Along with being scalped, since it looks like I forgot that one somehow.

The farther I descended, the more distant the sky seemed. I felt like I was leaving one domain—the rational world—and entering another. A darker, deeper world. I was once again entering a library.

Himalaya and Folsom's troops had outpaced me, and I could already hear gunfire below. Eventually I passed through a ring of melted glass and steel—the barrier Shasta had mentioned—and entered the Highbrary.

It was like a small city set inside an enormous cavern

---

* And those of you who aren't thinking this are instead thinking, *Hey, that's not what I was thinking.* See? I'm totally psychic.

with a very tall ceiling. I dangled above it all, amazed. I vaguely remembered learning that DC had been built on a swamp or something, but obviously that was a Librarian lie, considering this majestic stone cavern. It was so wide I couldn't make out the far edges, as they were too dark.

Light came from thousands of torches fluttering below, some being carried by Librarians—whom I made out as small figures beneath me. The cavern floor was clogged with buildings, most short but some stretching quite tall. The grim black buildings had an ancient feel to them and sat on different levels within the cavern, some on rocky outcroppings rising from the uneven cavern floor, others built in the middle of troughs beneath their fellows.

Among the buildings, the cavern was crisscrossed with bleak stone walkways. Librarians traversed these wearing red-and-black robes, the type you'd find for sale at Ye Olde Evil Cultist Clothing Emporium and Knife Shoppe™.

Near the center of the cavern, a short distance from me, one tall tower rose above the rest of the buildings. It was like a natural rock peak, with a flat top and steps around the outside.

It was capped by what appeared to be a stack of old books.

I didn't give that much heed, continuing my descent as

Grandpa and Draulin climbed down on their own ropes. Below, Himalaya's troops secured our landing site. Many of the Librarians nearby scattered, ducking into the cavern's numerous small buildings. As I continued down, I got a look into one of those; it was lined with bookshelves.

Archives. That made sense. Though as I neared the ground I was able to peek into a few more, and strangely some didn't hold books at all, but had shelves and shelves full of the oddest things. Stacks of coins, piles of wrappers, even rows of cereal boxes. The Librarians, it seemed, collected anything with writing on it. Maybe they were trying to re-create Alexandria.

I finally reached the bottom, my arms aching. Draulin landed next to me, not looking the least bit inconvenienced by the difficult climb. Stupid knights. Grandpa landed and wiped his brow, then reached up to help Cousin Dif, who was sweating profusely and looked a little the worse for wear from the climb down on the same rope as Grandpa.

We'd landed inside the area secured by Himalaya's Librarian freedom fighters, who fired on Librarian soldiers. Several of the other good Librarians threw handfuls of pamphlets to distract the cultist-looking Librarians scrambling for cover within our perimeter.

I ran for Himalaya, passing a group of cultist Librarians

huddled just inside one of the small archives. They seemed completely transfixed by a set of pamphlets.

"Should we be worried about them?" I asked.

"Nah," Himalaya said. "I made one word different on each of the pamphlets—they'll spend *at least* the next hour arguing how to properly index them."

"Neat," I said, stuffing a few pamphlets into my pocket. They were emblazoned with the phrase 615 EASY STEPS TO NOT BEING EVIL on the front.

Librarians fired back and forth, turning the area into a storm of gunfire. One of the rebels had dropped a crate down the hole and it had broken open, spilling teddy bears of various colors. I ran and snatched three, then pulled the pins and threw them in quick succession at approaching enemy troops.

Draulin tossed me another bear and the two of us took shelter beside my grandfather, who crouched next to a wall. "My, my . . ." Grandpa said, looking around the vast cavern. "This place is exactly as I imagined it. Nobbed Noviks! I've dreamed of breaking in here. Yes I have."

"Why aren't they fighting back very much?" I asked, pointing at the Librarians. The evil ones didn't seem to be mounting as strong an offense as I would have assumed. Sure, there was gunfire back toward us, but no explosions.

"They're probably worried about hurting the things in these archives," Draulin said.

"That might help Himalaya and her team hold out," I said.

"Yes, but for how long?" Draulin said. "Lord Smedry, have you given any thought toward how we are going to find one man in all of this?"

I nodded in agreement. This place *was* big, and my father was in here somewhere. Theoretically. We only had my mother's word on that fact. I'd used the Truthfinder's Lens to confirm she wasn't lying, but what if she was just plain wrong?

"We'll need to talk to your mother," Grandpa said, seeming troubled. Perhaps he was thinking along the same lines as I was. "She claimed she could find him."

"Let's get into one of these archive rooms," I said, tossing my bear. "Might be easier to chat without worrying about bullets." Draulin waved to Dif and to Shasta, who had just landed, and the five of us ducked into one of the hutlike stone archive rooms. Inside, shelves and shelves of recipe books shuddered against one another, responding to the firefight outside. A few robe-wearing cultists cowered in the corner, and I tossed a handful of pamphlets to keep them distracted.

"All right," Grandpa said to us. "Shasta, what do you suggest?"

"We find Attica," my mother said. "I'm sure he's here. This place holds one of the largest archives of Forgotten Language texts in existence. If we find where the Librarians are keeping those, we'll find him."

"Surely it's not that simple," I said. "I mean, how did *he* sneak in here? How is he keeping the Librarians from catching him? If he *is* here, he'll be hidden. What makes you think we'll be able to find him, if they can't?"

Draulin looked at me and blinked, as if stunned.

"What?" I demanded.

"I apologize, Lord Smedry," she said. "But that was merely a solid, responsible assessment of our situation—filled with insightful realizations and important questions that need to be asked."

Was that . . . a compliment?

"Of course," Draulin added, "a truly responsible person would have asked those things *before* leading us in a headfirst assault on the most powerful Librarian stronghold in the world. Baby steps, I suppose."

"Right," Grandpa said, clapping his hands. "So where are the Forgotten Language texts?"

My mother shrugged. "No idea. I've never been in here before, remember?"

An explosion shook the ground. I peeked out the doorway. Unfortunately, it looked like the Librarians had sent several hulking Alivened—made entirely from old romance novels—to attack our position. Thrown teddy bears reduced the first of these to fluttering scraps of paper, but more continued to come, and Alivened are surprisingly hardy.

"Himalaya!" I hissed.

She took a moment to pose dramatically in her cape and leather skirt before joining us. Being around Smedrys has that kind of effect on people.

"You all should go do your thing," she told us, shouldering her machine gun. "My people will pull into one of these buildings and hold off the Bibliodenites. We can probably hole up for a while. If it goes too long, I'm going to get my people out of here. We have grappling guns; we should be able to extract back out that hole."

"We need to find the archive of Forgotten Language texts," I said. "Any ideas?"

"I've never visited those," she said, "but these are Librarians. There's definitely an index in here *somewhere*. Find that, and it will lead you to the cavern with the Forgotten Language books."

"Okay," I said. "We'll just have to . . . Wait, did you say the *cavern* with the books? You mean the building inside *this* cavern, right?"

Himalaya laughed. "You think this is the whole High-brary? I already told you it's beneath the entire down-town! This is merely the central hub. There are hundreds upon hundreds of other caverns, though most are small—barely big enough for one subtopic—burrowed along corridors in the rock."

Great. "Well, Grandpa?"

"We split up, obviously!" Grandpa said. "Two groups; we'll search twice as quickly."

Searching infinity twice as fast didn't seem like it would get us anywhere, but Grandpa was still probably right. "I'll take Dif and Draulin," I said, reluctantly considering my options.

"I'm going with you," my mother said.

"But—"

"I came here at *your* request, not his," Shasta said, eyeing Grandpa. "Leavenworth can take the knight; his group will have only two people, so it makes sense for the knight to join him."

"Fine," I said.

"Lord Smedry," Draulin said. "I strongly recommend not separating me from the prisoner."

"What?" Shasta asked. "Worried you'll miss out on another chance to sucker punch me?"

The ground shook from another explosion.

"Make your decisions quickly, people," Himalaya said.

I met my mother's eyes, then pulled a Lens out of my pocket. I knew that some of the words she had said so far weren't lies, but there can be a big gap between "factually correct" and "true."

And so I raised the Shaper's Lens.

My grandfather drew in his breath sharply. He looked from me to Shasta. She didn't say a word, and I was confident she knew exactly what this Lens did. She knew a lot of things. Not quite as much as she pretended to know, mind you—but since she pretended to know basically everything, "not quite as much" still covered a lot of ground.

I raised the Lens and gave it a burst of power. As I'd been warned, I started glowing. The city's dome, which prevented people from using Lenses to disguise themselves and sneak in, made it obvious I was using a Lens—in this case, one that let me see someone's heart, soul, and deepest desires.

My mother's soul opened to me.

The air around her warped and seemed to burn away, revealing an image of her standing in the center of a peaceful street. On one side of her, suburban homes ran in a row, each with manicured grass and toys on the front porch.

Opposite them, Free Kingdomer castles rose with shining gates and beautiful brickwork. Everything seemed perfectly at peace, save my mother, who stood before a short stone column. It was about as tall as her waist, and Mother leaned against its top, hands pressed down on a blackness that seemed to be trying to bubble up through the center of the column.

Mother shoved and pushed, keeping the blackness inside. I suddenly heard a small voice crying, and watched my mother turn and look over her shoulder at a boy who stood in the street, arms outstretched. My mother reached toward him, and the blackness started to bubble out around her hand.

She turned her back on the child and continued to work, to toil, to keep that darkness contained. While all the while, the child cried out for his mother . . .

I found myself trembling, and so I ripped the Lens free of my eye and turned away. Stupid thing wasn't working. Wasn't it supposed to show me what my mother wanted most in life? This was obviously how she saw herself: a sole figure trying to keep the peace, to hold back destruction and darkness, at the cost of all else.

Well, that was merely *her* opinion. She wasn't the only one fighting. Far from it. She could have taken a little time for someone else in her life. What good did it do to save the world if the ones who needed you most were left to starve?

Shasta didn't offer me any comfort. She stood with arms folded, avoiding my eyes, as if uncomfortable.

I shoved the Lens away. Well, Grandpa *had* said it could be unpredictable. At least I had my answer. The Lens had shown me a world at peace, with the Hushlands and the Free Kingdoms existing side by side. That was what my mother wanted: a world where everyone could just live their lives. It was still terrible, as in her vision, the Librarians maintained their rule over half the world.

But at least I knew where her heart was.

Grandpa walked up to me and put his arm around my shoulders. I was taller than he was. It hadn't always been that way, had it?

"Strength, lad," he said softly.

The building rocked again. Right. Middle of a battle. Sneaking into the Highbrary. I composed myself and nodded to my grandfather, then back to the others. "I'll go with Mother and Cousin Dif," I said. "Grandpa Smedry will go with Draulin."

"Off we go, then!" Grandpa exclaimed. "To victory! Lad, you still have that phone Kaz gave you?"

I dug in my pocket, pulling it out. It was broken from one of my several falls.

"Drat," Grandpa said, then handed me his.

"But you—"

"We can communicate with Courier's Lenses," Grandpa said. "This is if you need to call Kaz or the rebel force here." He took another phone, Draulin's, and tossed it to Himalaya.

"And if you need to talk to them?" I demanded.

"I'll call you," Grandpa said lightly.

"Give me a report when you know how things are going," Himalaya said, pocketing the phone. "And I'll give you warning if my people have to retreat." She strode out to continue leading her force.

"Off with us, then!" Grandpa said.

"You go right, I'll go left?" I said to him.

"Sure," he said, then took me by the forearm and met my eyes, nodding once. "Good luck, lad."

I talk a lot about my grandpa in these volumes. I explain how impulsive, even reckless, he was. I discuss his force of personality and his sometimes bizarre actions.

But do not mistake my grandfather for a fool. His wisdom may not have been apparent, but I've never known a man as great as he was. As he bade me good luck, and as I looked into his eyes, I realized something.

"You're scared," I said to him.

"Terrified," he said. "The Librarians won't let the defeat at Mokia stand; the warmongers among them will push harder for a full-scale invasion of the Free Kingdoms, and your announcement will give them the fuel they need."

"So we screwed up?" I asked.

"Of course not," Grandpa said. "We fought, we struggled, and we did what we had to. But, well . . ."

"What?"

"Let's just say that there's a reason I was so keen to go along with an all-or-nothing infiltration of the Highbrary. We're in dangerous waters, lad. Dangerous waters indeed. And no Talents to keep us alive." He took a deep breath. "But keep your head up. We can get out of this yet. You find your father and stop him."

I frowned. "That makes it sound like you're not going to search for him."

"Oh, I'll keep my eyes open," Grandpa said. "But my path might lead another direction. We're in the Highbrary! Bleating Bears! I'll never have a better chance to sabotage the Librarian infrastructure. I'm going to destroy this place, if I can. So let's go give 'em hell!"

"Grandpa! This is a family story."

"Well, when you write this part down, simply tell everyone I said 'give them' with proper grammar." Eyes twinkling, he squeezed my arm.

With that, we parted.

Chapter

Melissa

Well, that last chapter was kind of self-important, wasn't it? I blame the relative lack of footnotes.* As a reward for being a good girl/boy/robot and reading all of that gobbledygook, I'm going to explain the chapter names to you. Never say I don't give you anything.†

You see, the chapters in this book are identified like they are to call attention to a growing problem in fiction, that of disrespect for chapters and their own individual desires. How would you like it if you didn't get to have a

---

* That's what I get for blowing an entire book's worth of footnote rations on the first one in the chapter.
† I mean, obviously I've given you lots of things during the course of this series. Granted, most were probably headaches.

name, but were instead assigned a number based on your order of creation? Instead of Samantha, Didgeridoo, or whatever silly name Hushlanders are using nowadays, what if you'd been named "Human Spawn Number One Hundred Eight Billion, Fourteen Million, Four Hundred Eighty Thousand and Two"?

I suspect you wouldn't like that. Well, chapters don't like it either. They never get to be themselves, you know? It's always "Chapter One" or "Chapter Twenty-Seven" or "Oh, When Is This Stupid Book Going to End?"

To bring attention to this, I've allowed the chapters to name themselves whatever they want. (All except Chapter Four; I put my foot down when he insisted he be allowed to have an extra *o* in the middle of his name.)

I dashed out into the firefight, Dif and Shasta right behind me. The good Librarian force had pulled back almost to the building we'd used for our impromptu conference. They'd taken casualties; this fight was real. I won't go into the gory details, but it wasn't pretty.

Angry, I pulled out the Shamefiller's Lens and pointed it at a group of oncoming Alivened monsters. I started glowing, and the Lens spurted out a ray of power.

My aim was off, and my beam hit the stone ground of the cavern.

"Oh, blast! I'm the worst section of floor ever! That

person just stubbed his toe on a bit of my uneven rock. And I wasn't washed properly! Their feet are going to totally get dirty walking upon me and—"

BOOOM.

Good enough, I thought as bits of burning paper fluttered down, bearing descriptions of bodices. A piece of me was amazed. Bastille had had trouble fighting *one* of these things, and I'd just taken out a group of them. Something was seriously wrong with my Oculator powers. I mean, it was awesomely wrong, yes, but the Lens I stuffed into my pocket was so hot to the touch it could have fired an egg.*

The explosion I caused made enough of a mess that my team was able to duck away from the main battlefield through a small alley between two archive buildings.

"So, Cousin!" Dif said. "What sort of zany, bombastic shenanigans do you have planned for us?"

"Find my dad," I said, looking to Shasta. "How do we get an index for this place?"

"Only the most important of Librarians will have that kind of information," Shasta said. "If this is like other high-level libraries, they'll carry something called an authenticator. It will let them into important rooms, and probably will include a map and copies of the local indexes."

---

* Bad egg! You can't work here anymore.

"So we need to steal one of those," I said, rubbing my chin. "Or convince a Librarian to lead us where we want to go."

"Yeah, yeah!" Dif said. "And along the way, we'll do something *really* unexpected and silly, right? Then, as we go farther, it will suddenly make perfect sense!"

Why had I put him in my team again?

"Wouldn't the lesser Librarians need the index?" I asked as we continued down the alleyway. "How else would they know where to go?"

"Lesser Librarians," my mother said, "get assigned to one of these small buildings and spend their entire lives working inside it—adding new items when brought, designing new sorting methods when they have nothing to do. They'll never know the entire Highbrary's index; that's a holy thing beyond them. And they're unlikely to have authenticators that will get us past locked doors."

I shivered, thinking of a life trapped in a little room far from the sun, doing menial, repetitive work. It would be like . . . well, like any other job, I guess.* But those robes sure did look hot.

Robes . . .

---

* Except being a lion wrestler. But I hear the overtime for that job is killer.

As we left the alleyway, I led the others around the corner and into another of the archive rooms. This one was filled with shelves and shelves of those little rules inserts you get with a deck of playing cards. Not the playing cards themselves, mind you. Just the rules.

This place was odder than a river-dwelling species of mammal from the mustelidae family.*

Inside were a handful of the robe-wearing cultist Librarians. These, instead of cowering, were calmly moving stacks of cards and holding each one up to a candle's flame to inspect it.

"Indexing the cards by minor variations in translucence," my mother explained. "Hopscotch Vindaloo scale."

I stepped up to the Librarians and put on my Oculator's Lenses, trying my best to look threatening. "Ladies and gentlemen, I'm going to need everyone in this room to remove their clothing."

The Librarians kept right on working, though Cousin Dif shrugged and began to unbutton his shirt.

"Not you," I said.

"Technically, you did say—"

---

* Made ya look that one up, didn't I?

"Ahem," I said more loudly, getting out my Shamefiller's Lens, then stepping toward the working Librarians. "Don't make me use this!"

They barely glanced at me.

"These are archivists, Alcatraz," my mother said, brushing past me. "You're making the wrong kind of threats; personal safety is of little concern to these types." She snatched a rules card off a table and held it toward a candle.

"No!" one of the Librarians cried. "Only one million seven hundred thousand and sixty-three of those were printed! It's irreplaceable!"

"Plus," another added, "that one has a smudge on the left side. It's a *misprint!*"

"Robes," my mother said, "on the floor. Now."

They hurried to obey. Under the dark robes they wore surprisingly normal clothing. Slacks, blouses or polo shirts. Business-casual dress. I suddenly imagined how life must be for these Librarians, who were otherwise ordinary people from the Hushlands. In the mornings they'd kiss their spouses, then drive off to work in a secret underground bunker where they sorted playing cards all day for a sect of evil Librarians.

We quickly threw the robes on over our other clothing.

"Hey," one of the Librarians said to me, "you look

familiar. Are you from section seven, Wardens of the Standard?" It was disturbing that she was a teenager not much older than me. I'd always envisioned all Librarians as super old. Like, in their *thirties.*

I kept working as the girl inspected me. My face might pose a problem, seeing as how I'd sort of appeared on every glass surface in the world.*

"I've got it," the Librarian girl said. "We met at last year's Christmas ball and infidel burning. Right?"

I looked at her, and she tapped her chin, then grew suddenly pale. "Oh," she said, then apparently realized why we might be stealing her clothing. *"Oh!"*

Mother clocked her. Like, Shasta hit the girl upside the head, knocking her out cold. This finally made the other Librarians worry for their safety, and they scrambled away, hiding behind bookshelves.

"Mother!" I said.

Shasta shrugged. "Best to be safe. Let's go."

I couldn't really complain—we were at war, after all— but that still didn't seem appropriate. The Librarian girl was basically a civilian.

The robes I had put on didn't fit—but that didn't mat-

------

* Whoops.

ter, since they didn't fit the Librarians either. When we left the room, we were well disguised.*

Once again out in the main cavern, we ducked our heads and scuttled away, pretending to be Librarians who were frightened by the firefight. Himalaya's group had pulled back into the one building and were fighting furiously, isolated and trapped. How would they escape? Would they become another casualty of Smedry recklessness?

---

* The only way we could have done it better is if we'd been wearing ropes, a bucket, and a sign that said TOSS IN A COIN FOR A WISH.

Perhaps it was the way that Cousin Dif bounced forward—eager to be on with the infiltration—but I suddenly saw us as the others must. Always stumbling into things, causing a ruckus, then only escaping because our Talents kept us alive. No wonder Draulin griped so much.

We wound through the Highbrary's main cavern, heads down. This place was extraordinarily elaborate, with stone pathways rising high in the air, forming bridges that wrapped around smaller archive buildings. Everything had a natural look to it, like the stone had just happened to grow that way, although the whole was far too impressive to have been the product of random chance. (Kind of like my ego.)

"So we have to find a high-level Librarian," I hissed to my mother. I made sure to keep the hood down over my face to prevent anyone else from identifying me.

"It seems our best bet."

"How will we recognize them?"

"It should be easy."

"You're sure?"

"I'm sure."

"I'm not."

"I'm Dif!"

We both looked at him.

"Well I *am*," Dif said, sullen, as we crossed an arching

stone bridge, traveling deeper into the cavern. To my right that spindly tower of rock—the one I'd seen when climbing down from above—reached toward the ceiling. It gave me chills to look at it, and I turned away.

As we drew closer to the outer wall of the cavern, I could see the side tunnels Himalaya had mentioned: they were grand, wide things burrowed into the stone away from this main cavern. Librarians scuttled in and out like ants; many seemed to be carrying on with their normal work despite the battle.

I had an inkling that we needed to get out of the main cavern. Too many peons were doing normal work here. If we wanted to find Librarians like Blackburn or She Who Cannot Be Named, we'd want to look for more exclusive areas. Important people don't like to be forced to associate with their inferiors.*

I turned us toward one of the tunnels. My mother huffed, as she'd just turned the other direction. "I should be in control here," she told me. "You don't know where you're going."

"Neither do you. You said you've never been in here before."

---

* For example, exactly how often have you seen me on book tour?

"I know general Librarian architecture."

"Then where should we look?"

"We won't find any Dark Oculators or high-ranking Wardens of the Standard in here," my mother said. "We'll need to look someplace more isolated, more exclusive."

"Like, say, down that tunnel I pointed us toward."

My mother ground her teeth. "You," she said, "are insufferable."

"And after all the wonderful parenting you did too. Who would have thought?"

"That was uncalled for," she said. "If we're going to work together, we obviously need to establish some ground rules."

"Remember that a GFCI is required for all receptacles in wet locations, as per National Electric Code," Dif said, raising a finger.

"Not that type of ground rule,"* my mother snapped. She looked to me. "Rule One: You and I need to at least *try* to get along."

"I can accept that," I said.

"Good. Rule Two: I don't do what you say."

---

* You are following along with this chapter's puns, right? Well, if they're too highbrow for you, don't worry. There's a fart joke coming soon.

"Great," I said. "I hereby instruct you to keep breathing."

"You are *so* annoying."

"Is that Rule Three?"

"It's a law of the universe," Mother said, throwing her hands into the air. "You can insult my parenting if you wish, but I *did* try to see that this didn't happen!"

"And I'm so sorry to disappoint,"* I said.

"But," my mother continued, "I don't know what I expected, considering your father."

"I doubt I inherited my most annoying attributes one hundred percent completely from him."

"You certainly did, you little mongrel."

"Mongrel? As in, a mixed breed of questionable parentage?"

My mother paused. "Huh. Yeah."

"Rule Three," I said. "It's unwise to slander someone's parentage if, in fact, *you* are their parent."

"I can accept that," my mother said. "Rule Four: Never mention this conversation, or my part in it, to anyone."

"Rule Five," Dif added. "Even if you think you can do it softly, never pass gas in a crowded room unless the music is really loud. Better to be safe."

---

* You're a terrible point! Not pointy at all! And your mother smells like a wet sheep.

We both glared at him.

"I learned that one the hard way, I'll tell you."

"Rule Six," I began.

"Wait, no," Mother said. "You're *not* going to let that stand as Rule Five, are you?"

"Do you think it's false?"

"No. It's just crude."*

"Rule Six," I continued. "I get to choose how to deal with my father. Not you."

"I can't accept that," she said.

"You have to. It's not negotiable. If you don't agree, we'll split up right here, Dif and I going one way, you going the other. I won't lead you to him unless you're willing to let me make the decision."

"I'm his wife!"

"You're his enemy."

"So are you."

"No," I said as we rounded a corner between two small archive buildings. "I haven't decided what I am yet. At the very least I want to talk to him before we do anything."

"I can't believe you—"

She cut off and we stopped in place. We'd been making

---

* Like that's ever stopped us before. Remember the pig butt incident?

our way toward the tunnel at the side of the chamber, but hadn't noticed the large group of Librarian soldiers gathering here beside the chamber wall.

A tall Librarian woman in a black robe looked toward us. Her jet-black hair was woven within a silver hairnet, and a pair of light-red reading glasses dangled from a chain around her neck. Oculator's Lenses.

This woman was at least a foot taller than even the soldiers. Pale skin. Black lipstick. Yeah, Mom was right. I recognized a high-ranking Librarian immediately upon seeing her—and worse, this one was apparently a Dark Oculator.

"Ah," she said. "You three don't look busy. Gather weapons. We have work to do."

We gawked at her.

"Now!" she snapped, pointing toward a row of swords along the wall. Reluctantly we moved to obey. Fleeing now, in defiance of an order, would only bring this entire crew of fifty soldiers chasing after us.

"Rule Seven," Cousin Dif muttered as we selected weapons. "From now on, you two spend a little less time arguing about who's in charge and a little more time paying attention to where you're shattering leading us!"

You may have noticed my use of puns in the last chapter. I mean, I pointed them out pretty blatantly, so if you didn't notice, it means you aren't paying attention as you read. And in that case, you should

AAAAAAAAAAAAAAAAAAAAAAAAAAAAAA-
AAAAAAAAAAAAAAAAAAAAAAAAAAAAAA-
AAAAAAAAAAAAAAAAAAAAAAAAAAAAAA-
AAAAAAAAAAAAAAAAAAHHHHHHHHHHH-
HHHHHHHHHHHHHHHHHHHHHHHHHHHHH-
HHHHHHHHHHHHHHHHHHHHHHHHHHHHH-
HHHHHHHHHHHHHHHHHHHHHHHHHHHHH-
HHHHHHHHHHHHHHHHHHHHHHHHHHHHH-
HHHH!!

Awake now? Good! Now, those of you who were sleepy,

go reread that last chapter, because it was really clever and I don't want you to miss any of it. The rest of you, let's talk about puns.*

Puns are obviously the highest form of literary genius that an author can display. Shakespeare used puns, and we all know he invented every word in the English language. I mean, before that guy we were all speaking French or something. (Which was super inconvenient, since France doesn't actually exist and neither does its language. So I imagine all interactions between people went something like what you saw in Chapter Alice. You may commence shuddering in horror at that idea.)

Yeah. So, here's a tip for you. Use a lot of puns in your writing. That way, when someone complains that your book isn't entertaining enough—or that it makes too many self-indulgent deviations into meaningless explanations of writing techniques—you can point out your use of brilliant puns to conclusively prove that they are an ignorant savage or something.

We lined up with the other Librarians, awkwardly carrying swords and shields, still wearing our robes as disguises. We weren't the only minor Librarians the

---

* And to define this for those of you who prefer the fart jokes, a "pun" is a joke where you say one thing, but you mean a mother.

Dark Oculator had recruited; fully half the group lining up here wore awkward-fitting robes like ours and were the type of people who seemed better suited to unsplicing commas than cutting out enemy spleens.

I glanced at my mother, who—in the shuffling as the Librarians formed marching lines—had been pushed back two rows from me. She nervously tugged the hood of her robe down farther; I wasn't the only recognizable one in our team. Dif did likewise on my right, but I wasn't too worried about him.

Did I have a Lens that would get us out of this? I fished in the pocket of my robe, where I'd deposited my Lenses. Shaper's Lens, Truthfinder's Lens, Courier's Lenses, basic Oculator's Lenses, and the Shamefiller's Lens. I wasn't about to begin blowing people up with that last one—far too messy—and the others would be too slow to use in any realistic way. Using one would reveal me to the Dark Oculator.

That's not all that could give me away, I realized uncomfortably, glancing again at the reading glasses hanging around the woman's neck. If she put those on, I'd glow like a Christmas tree; another Oculator is easily spotted by one of our kind who is looking.

My every instinct screamed at me to get out of this line of troops and hide. At the same time she was exactly what

I'd been searching for—a high-ranking Librarian with access to the more hidden parts of the Highbrary. What I really needed to do was find a way to disable the other fifty troops, capture this woman, then intimidate her into giving me her index.

Right. Piece of cake.*

The Dark Oculator, fortunately, didn't put on her Lenses. Instead she led us all in a march around the outside perimeter of the main cavern. I glanced toward Dif, or where I thought Dif had been standing. Instead there was an awkward-looking young Librarian youth with pimples and braces. I did catch a glimpse of a dark Librarian robe swooshing as it ducked to the side of a building we passed.

Shattering Glass! How had he managed to escape so easily? Had that been his Talent? Might have been; I didn't remember seeing him leave. I still needed to talk to him about that. If I could find out why his was working and the rest weren't, I might be able to figure out what was going on.

---

* For you Free Kingdomers reading this book, that's a Hushlander phrase that means, roughly, "This will be really easy, except I'm probably using the phrase sarcastically, so it's not going to be easy at all." I have no idea why cake is involved, except for the fact that cake is great, so why *not* involve it? Really, more sayings should involve cake.

I glanced back at my mother, who was still in line. She watched that Dark Oculator, probably thinking—as I had—that this would be an excellent chance to get the information we needed. Assuming we didn't *also* end up with a lot of "being killed" we didn't need.

"I'm a terrible robe," a voice whispered in my head. "I have spots of mustard all over my hem. Oh, why couldn't I be cleaner?"

What in the cake? I fiddled in my pocket, looking for my Shamefiller's Lens.

"We're going to fight those people who broke in," the boy next to me said.

I started. Had he been talking to me? But no, an older Librarian marching beside him replied. "I doubt it," the man said. "I have a cousin who does archives on the soda cans near there, and *he* says that they're keeping underlings away. Something about dangerous literalogical warfare being employed."

I searched desperately in my pocket as my robe kept talking, sounding more and more ashamed. My fingers brushed one of my Lenses, and it had grown warm to the touch.

It had activated without my direct command. I wasn't glowing yet—that was good—but the fact that the Lens was acting on its own seemed like a very, *very* bad precedent.

"I'll bet we've been recruited to go do something about those ghosts," said a woman behind us.

"The . . . ghosts?" asked the boy beside me. "That's a rumor."

"Nope," the woman said, and she seemed to take delight in saying it. "Didn't you hear? They've been sending initiates to the Library of Alexandria, forcing them to give up their souls for books, then towing them back here to interrogate them on what they learned."

"That's not it," said the older Librarian man. "They've found a way to transport books from the Library of Alexandria here *without* making someone touch them. They use some kind of robot that the old spirits don't know how to react to, so they can't punish anyone for moving the volumes. Instead, they've come here to guard their tomes. *That's* why people keep seeing them around."

Great. Undead Librarians too? This infiltration was getting more and more fun by the moment. I latched on to my Shamefiller's Lens, forcing it—with effort—to power down. As it grew cool to my touch, I let out a relieved breath. Having my robe suddenly explode with me still in it seemed like a very embarrassing way to die. I added it to my list.*

---

* Besides, I really didn't want to make a habit of vaporizing my own clothing. Once in a series is my limit.

"I . . ." the young Librarian said, then gulped. "I still think the ghosts are rumors."

"Think what you want, Kyle," the woman said. "Doesn't change the truth." Someone nudged me in the back. "What about you? Have you seen them?"

"Uh . . ." I said. "Nope. Haven't seen them."

The youth looked at me, peering into my hood, which had slipped back a little. "Hey. You're not from our sector."

"The Oculator grabbed him and his team last-minute," the older Librarian man said. "What are you guys? Card runners?"

"Yeah," I said. "But I'm new."

"Did we train together?" the youth asked. "You look familiar to me. . . ."

Oh, cake.

"Yeah, we did," I said. "But I got moved out of training quickly."

"I—"

"You back there!" the Oculator in front snapped. "Quiet!"

Never had I been so happy to be shushed by a Librarian. Fortunately, the youth seemed to lose interest in interrogating me—instead growing nervous as we approached a large side tunnel that, unlike the others, didn't have people flowing in and out of it.

Our group stopped at the mouth of this tunnel: a deep passage of rock, lined at the sides with oil lamps in the shape of metal skulls with the fire coming out of their upturned mouths. They stared at the ceiling, eye holes gaping, like doomed souls.*

Bestial roars echoed down that hallway. Terrible screeches, along with thumping and the sound of claws on rock. The Librarians around me huddled closer together and held out swords. Some real Librarian soldiers—beefy men in bow ties, suspenders, and plaid shirts that barely contained their muscles—stood just inside the tunnel. It didn't look like *they* were going to have to fight whatever was in there; the Dark Oculator had intentionally gathered up expendable troops.

"All right, people," the woman said to us. "We need you to do a little reconnaissance. Go in, figure out what is making that noise, and report back. Bring me its head and you'll be richly rewarded."

Another roar echoed in the hallway, a sound like a lion being eaten by a dragon during a heavy metal concert. Whatever else happened, I *couldn't* let myself be sent in to fight that thing. I needed to talk to this Dark Oculator, get information out of her, and . . .

---

* Librarians really *do* have a flare for dramatic scenery. Rutabaga.

And I started as I realized she'd put on her Oculator's Lenses to peer down the darkened corridor. She apparently didn't see anything interesting through her Lenses, for she turned lazily back toward us to give another order.

She stopped mid-word as she saw me.

I pulled down the front of my hood to obscure my face, then ducked out of the line and strode toward the front of the group, dragging the big sword I'd been given as a weapon. My mother had moved up in the line to look down the corridor, and as I passed she hissed at me, "What are you doing?"

There was no time to explain. I stepped right up to the Dark Oculator. "I believe I am in the wrong place," I said, speaking with a rasping voice. "I was upon another mission when you pulled me into your team. I came along out of curiosity, but I must now be away."

"Who are you?" the woman snapped. "Too much power . . . What Lenses are you holding?" She reached for the front of my hood, to pull it back and reveal my face.

I slapped her hand away. "I come on the authority of the Scrivener himself, and have power beyond your imagining. That is all you need know."

"The Scrivener!" the woman said. She glanced at the other troops, then whispered to me, "Finally! Where has Lord Biblioden gone? What has he been doing? We haven't seen him in the Highbrary in weeks!"

I gulped. So it was true. Someone claiming to be Biblioden had been here in the Highbrary leading the Librarians.

"That is none of your concern," I hissed.

"He gave you Lenses," the woman said. "Is his plan succeeding, then?"

"I . . ." Plan? "Sure. Of course it is. My awe-inspiring power should be proof enough for one such as you."

She studied me, squinting, and I hoped the gloom would keep her from seeing my face within the hood.

"Awe-inspiring power," the woman said.

"Yup."

"Stronger than I am?"

"Most certainly."

"Great," the woman said, pointing down the tunnel. "Then *you* can go deal with that."

"Uh . . . No, too busy. Too much to do. I need you to direct me toward the room with the Forgotten—"

"If you *have* been sent by the Scrivener," the woman said, "you'll know about the Code of Irrevocability."

"Uh . . ."

"And since there are valuable texts that direction," the woman continued, "you'll know that you *have* to go and rescue them. By the oath of all Librarians."

She looked satisfied, as if she'd won the argument. Which was probably true, in the same way that you'll likely win any argument you have with a lump of coal. I had no idea what we'd just talked about.

But it seemed that I didn't have much choice.

Another roar echoed in the corridor.

"I need to get to the Forgotten Language texts," I said stubbornly.

"Then I will take you," the woman said. "As soon as the immediate threat is dealt with." She stepped back from me and turned toward the troops. "Looks like we have a volunteer to go deal with the danger on his own. Unfortunately, the rest of you won't be able to participate."

"Oh," said one of the Librarians, looking disappointed. "Are you sure we can't go and—?"

He yelped as the others nearby knocked him off his feet and several piled on top of him.

"Never mind what I just said," a voice said from the pile, obviously someone else imitating the guy. "We're good waiting. Happy to let someone else have the opportunity. Not selfish at all."

Everyone looked toward me. In the group, my mother shook her head and raised her hand to her brow.

"Sure," I said. "I'll go deal with the unspeakable horror on my own. Be right back."

The Librarians waited expectantly. So, with a sigh of resignation, I started down the corridor alone, dragging my too-big sword behind me.

Chapter

° Shu Wei °

Not long now.

I keep thinking of ways I could slow this down. I've changed my mind. Instead of getting me that sandwich, I want you to go find a big thick epic fantasy novel. Or a dictionary. Basically, anything boring with lots of words in it that would take forever to read.

You got that? Good. Now hit me over the head with it. Maybe if I have a concussion I'll forget about what's coming in a few chapters.

I walked slowly down the corridor, drawing closer and closer to those horrible sounds. Was this the ghost that the Librarians had been talking about? It seemed far too noisy for that, but what did I know?

Another blast of angry roaring washed over me. My

already slow step grew increasingly hesitant. This is your real "hero," my dear readers. This is my true self. Lots of bluster, lots of talk of being a Smedry and charging forward recklessly. But when confronted with a real danger, I found myself terrified.

A coward.

I heard footsteps on the stone behind and—grateful for any excuse to look away from the darkness ahead—I glanced back. Was help coming?

No, it was only Dif.

He scuttled up the tunnel toward me, a cloaked, spindly figure I identified because of his height. Several Librarians behind called to him, saying, "There's no need!" and "Let that other guy get eaten first!" But ever a stalwart Smedry, Dif ignored them, joining me, grinning beneath his hood.

"Couldn't let you have all the fun on your own, Cousin!" he exclaimed. "Why throw one Smedry into the pit of doom when you can throw two!"

I suddenly felt an overwhelming sense of relief—and affection—for my cousin. The guy was over-the-top, but he'd come to join me when nobody else would. Beyond that, he was *family*. I'd decided this was where I belonged—anywhere another Smedry could be found. Merely having him nearby strengthened me, made me

Oh THIS would have ended well...
—Bastille

turn back toward the darkness and start striding forward again.

"So, what do you suppose it is?" Dif asked. "Rampaging super-wombat? Draco-zombi-thulhu? Professional wrestlers watching daytime television? A nest of mutated crocodiles who have been fed a steady diet of Smedry blood, trained to someday be unleashed so they can flay our skin from our bones and chew our skulls to powder?"

Another roar shook the walls.

"You're not making this any less nerve-racking, Dif," I muttered.

"Sorry."

Eventually we got far enough from the entrance to the tunnel that I couldn't see the pack of Librarians waiting behind. But before we reached the source of the sounds, the ground fell away into a vast pit spanned by a long rope bridge. The roars were definitely coming from the other side.

"Why in the world," I said, "would there be a *pit* in the middle of the tunnel?"

"Oh, Librarians are always building things like this," Dif said, stepping onto the rope bridge. "Bottomless pits in the middle of rooms, tunnels and shafts to nowhere. They think it makes everything feel more evil."

I watched him start across the bridge, which swung

leisurely in a breeze from somewhere. The walls here had
been carved with reliefs depicting Librarians kneeling
before a figure I could only imagine was Biblioden. The
ceiling opened up like the floor did, stretching into darkness. Shouldn't the surface have been up there? Washington, DC? I saw no signs of sunlight.

I edged my way onto the bridge. Why hadn't I put
"death by falling off a rope bridge into a bottomless pit"
on my list?

Wouldn't this be a fitting end? All this work, all these
books, just to have me slip and fall to my doom.

The end.

As great a joke as that would have been on you, it didn't happen.*

I shoved down my cowardice and carefully followed Dif across the swinging bridge. I could make out some kind of *wub-wub-wub* sound coming from below. It was hard to hear over those roars, but it was distinct once I noticed it.

---

* Nothing really to say here. Just felt like I needed a footnote. So, uh, how's your family doing?

I stopped on the bridge and peered down into the depths. Although the only light came from those tiny oil lamps on the walls, I thought I caught a glimmer of something spinning down below. The breeze was stronger here; something was pulling air downward.

"Fans?" I asked, looking toward Dif.

"Probably their ventilation system," he said, sweeping his hand around dramatically. "This is an archive! These tunnels need a mighty fine set of fans to blow dry air into the rooms to keep things from getting moldy."

I nodded, thinking of how vast an undertaking it must have been to build this place. This open shaft above us was an air inlet, and the fans below were pulling wind down into the ventilation system.

Dif backed up a few steps until he was next to me on the bridge. He leaned out—much too far, in my opinion—looking down into the pit.

Man, I thought, *Bastille would hate this place.* She has this thing about heights. And by "thing" I mean "incredible, soul-clutching terror." I think it's because she hasn't figured out a way she can stab "heights" yet.

Another roar seemed to make the entire bridge shake. "So, how *are* we going to deal with that whatever-it-is?" Dif asked.

"I still have this sword," I said, holding the thing up.

"Ever used one of those?"

"Nope."

"Perfect. Much more dramatic." Dif grinned a Smedry grin, leaning out farther over the shaft. "Wow. Check out those carvings on the wall!"

If Dif thought the sword was a good idea, then it was probably a terrible one. Instead I fished in my robe pocket, bringing out one of my Lenses. This was my Truthfinder's Lens, the one Alcatraz the First had left behind so I could discern the lies from the truths. "I just have to use Lenses on the monster, whatever it is."

And after that, I'd use them on my father. With my Truthfinder's Lens, I could know for certain what he intended.

"Wow!" Dif said, sweeping the other direction to point at the other wall. "More murals over there!" And as he moved, he accidentally smacked his hand into mine.

The Truthfinder's Lens tumbled from my fingers.

I cried out, dropping to my knees on the precarious bridge. I reached for my Lens, but it bounced once off a wooden slat and rolled off the bridge. I watched as it flipped in the air, plummeting like a single raindrop down, down, down into blackness.

I heard a faint *crack* as it hit the enormous spinning fans.

I knelt there, wide-eyed, feeling a crushing sense of loss. No. Not *that* Lens! I . . . I . . .

"Oh!" Dif said. "Oh, I'm so sorry!" He dropped to his knees beside me, looking down at the blackness. "We can get it, Cousin. We cut the ropes of the bridge, dropping us down while we cling to the wooden boards. No, it's not long enough. We slice up the ropes on the bridge and make a way to climb down . . . into a bunch of spinning death-fans that probably already destroyed the Lens anyway. . . ."

His face fell.*

I stared after the Lens for a long moment, but I knew there was nothing we could do now. Later, once our job was done here, I could try to get down there and gather the shards so my grandfather could reforge the Lens.

"I'm so, *so* sorry," Dif said. "That . . . that wasn't very Smedry-like, was it? It was spontaneous, I mean, but . . ." He looked sick.

I was immediately angry with him. Hateful, even. Then I thought of all the things I'd broken in my life, all the mistakes I'd made. With effort, I shoved down my annoyance, then stood and reached to help him to his feet.

------

* Not going to make a pun here. Way too obvious. You've gotta be sneaky with them.

"It's all right," I said. "We all make mistakes."

He lit up, nodding enthusiastically. He *was* earnest. He was also a buffoon, but hey, he wasn't the one who had accidentally warned the entire world he was going to be sneaking into the Highbrary.

"Come on," I said, shouldering the sword and striding across the bridge. "I'm tired of wondering what type of deadly monster is waiting to devour us."

On the other side, I was relieved to step onto solid ground again. This larger tunnel was set with rooms at the sides, and glancing in one I saw shelves upon shelves of books. It looked like the huts in the central chamber mainly kept things like soda cans and license plates, while these deeper chambers had the actual books.

The sounds were very close now. I inched along, back to the wall, approaching a doorway to my left. Yup. That was where the sounds were coming from.

I looked at Dif, and we both took a deep breath. Then we charged into the room, me with my sword out, him with his fists up as if fully prepared to punch the living daylights out of the draco-zombi-thulhu, whatever that is. Instead, we were confronted by an enormous tyrannosaurus rex with blood dripping from its teeth.

"Oh," I said, relaxing immediately. "Thank goodness."

Chapter

15

I've been thinking.

Maybe my life *is* a fable, of the kind Aesop wrote. The purpose of those was to warn. He told an entertaining story that, at the end, proved a point. *That's* why all those animals got eaten, mangled, beheaded, crushed, and defenestrated.*

My life is not just a story—but simply because this all happened doesn't mean you can't learn something. It's obvious to me now. Maybe there *is* a point to all this! You *are* supposed to learn something from it!

Never let your chapters choose their own names. It makes things terribly confusing.

---

* What? You haven't heard the fable of the rat who got tossed out of a window? It's very popular among wooly sea sloths.

The dinosaur roared again, throwing back its head, shaking the walls with the ferocity of its anger.

"Cheers, Alcatraz!" said a pterodactyl* sitting at a little table in the room. He wore a vest and trousers, and was sipping tea from a small cup.

"Hey, Charles," I said, waving Dif into the room, then peeking out to see that no Librarians were near. "What's up with Douglas?"

"Bit my lip!" said the T. rex.

"Really?" I said, setting the sword by the door and pulling a handkerchief out of my pocket.† "That hardly seems worth all of this noise."

"Don't mind him, good chap," said Charles the pteradactyl.‡ "He merely has a very low threshold for pain and a very high propensity for making a brilliant racket!"

"That's terribly unfair," Douglas said. "Have you *seen* these teeth of mine? A bit lip is no trivial matter, I say!" In truth, he was small for a T. rex. Barely taller than a human adult, but he still had to lean down so that I could dab at the blood on his teeth.

A few other dinosaurs sat at the table with Charles.

---

* Huh. First try. What are the odds?
† All good tuxes come with one.
‡ That's more like it.

I'd met Margaret, the duck-billed dinosaur, along with Charles and Douglas during my first library incursion with my grandfather. I didn't know the last of the group, a dinosaur that had four horns—but also a long pointed face. I'm fairly certain the business suit with a skirt meant she was female, but I'd never seen her species in a textbook.

Dif regarded the dinosaurs with a sneer that he obviously tried to cover up when I glanced at him. Like Bastille, he didn't seem to think much of them. Personally, I was more than happy to find friendly faces—even reptilian ones—instead of some eldritch monster thirsting to drink my soul.

"What are you guys doing here?" I asked. "Didn't you learn your lesson last time?" The Librarians liked to kill dinosaurs and stick their bones in museums.

"We're field researchers," Charles said indignantly. "We can't do important work in a stuffy university."

"Stuffy libraries are much better," Megan the duck-billed dinosaur agreed.

"Besides!" said the T. rex. "We couldn't let you come here alone, good chap!"

I groaned. "So you saw my speech too?"

"'It's time for you to stop whining!'" Charles proclaimed, raising his teacup. "'And either help or get out of my way!' Very dramatic. Set the Librarians *all* abuzz."

"They knew I was coming for them," I said with a sigh, sitting down with the dinosaurs and eating a few of their British-style cookie things.*

"Yes, yes," said the not-triceratops. "But that's not what made the Librarians so upset. Not merely your arrival, but your speech. Don't you realize what you said? It was incredible, extraordinary, spectacular!"

The dinosaurs looked at me expectantly. Hopefully the Librarians outside in the hallway would think I was fighting in here or something. This particular hall of books didn't seem to have any archivists in it at the moment.

"Your speech," Charles prompted. "You said, 'I know something the Librarians don't.' The Librarians have gone crazy trying to figure out what it is!"

"I was talking about my determination," I said. "It was a metaphor. 'I'm stronger than they think.' Something like that." I shrugged. I didn't really remember what I'd said all that well; it had just kind of come out.†

---

* Yes, dinosaurs are English—or, rather, English people sound like folks from Northern Nalhalla, where most of the dinosaur cities can be found. So if you met them, they'd sound and act British to you. As opposed to Smedrys, who generally just sound and act Bratish.

† Yes, I know that speech has been recorded as one of the most influential ever spoken. Unlike what your textbooks say, I didn't spend three weeks preparing it. Sorry to destroy any illusions you have about me.

"Well," Douglas said, flopping down beside the table near me, "they certainly *thought* you meant something by it. So we couldn't sit back and let all this happen!"

"Well, I suppose we can use all the soldiers we can get," I said.

"Soldiers?" Charles the ptterodactyl asked.

"Militants," the not-triceratops explained. "Combatants, fighters, warriors."

"I know what it means, Mary," Charles said. "I was simply surprised. Uh . . . we're not exactly the fighting type, Lord Alcatraz."

"But you just said—"

"We're here," Margaret said, raising her cup, "because this is a fantastic opportunity to explore Hushlander reactions to extreme stress!"

"Do you have any idea how many papers we could write about this?" the four-horned dinosaur said. "Essays, dissertations, treatises!"

"Librarian homeland besieged?" Charles said. "Smedrys running around in the Highbrary, having a bash at bringing down the entire place? This will be *golden*."

But if you're this far into my autobiography, I figure you must have defenestrated those long ago.

"Marvelous," the not-triceratops said, "engaging, fascinating, wonderful."*

"Oh," I said. "I was hoping you'd help."

"Well," Charles added, "we did have Douglas eat the *M* section in the fiction archive. That might sow a little chaos."

"Honestly," Douglas said, "sparkles? Hasn't she ever *met* any undead?"

"Alcatraz," Dif said, "we should get back. The Dark Oculator might send one of those poor fools outside to come look for us." He'd refused the seat I'd pulled out for him, and stood by the doorway, arms folded.

"Yeah, all right," I said, rising. "I don't suppose you guys could create a ruckus in here for a few minutes, make it sound like I'm fighting you?"

The dinosaurs grew silent.

"Like . . . acting?" Margaret asked.

"Performing!" the not-triceratops said. "Playing, portraying!"

"I don't know about that," Charles said. "Did anyone here take any classes in theatre?"

"What?" Douglas demanded. "And mingle with the unwashed cretins in the *humanities* department?"

"Please?" I asked. "The Librarians have to think I

---

* Have you figured out what kind of dinosaur she is yet?

destroyed whatever monster was in here. Otherwise they'll come peeking in and discover you."

The dinosaurs sighed, then rose. "Very well," Margaret said. "Though I don't like interfering in the social experiment environment that you provide here, young Smedry."

They stared at each other for a moment.

Then they started roaring. I was shocked by the ferocity of it, and stumbled back, my eyes widening. For all their complaints, they quickly got into the act, screeching, bellowing, and making such a racket I could barely hear myself cake.*

I stepped up to Dif. "Probably best if we wait," I told him over the racket. "Let them assume we're fighting."

He nodded, holding his ears and glaring at the dinosaurs. Shattering Glass. His dislike of them exceeded even Bastille's. I shook my head and decided to spend a few minutes looking through this archive room. It was filled with rows and rows of books—every one of which appeared to be a biography of a stenographer. I'd had no idea that people *wrote* biographies of stenographers, let alone that there were enough to fill dozens upon dozens of shelves. Honestly, I barely knew what a stenographer was.

---

* Okay, so maybe "cake" doesn't work as a replacement in every phrase. I guess that idea turned out to be half-baked.

The Librarians kept everything immaculately clean, but none of these books seemed *read*. Their spines were too perfect, the pages pristine. What was the point of all this? Wasn't information supposed to be used?

At the back of the room I found a small table with a chair by it, as if placed as a reluctant concession to the idea that someone might someday come here and violate these books by actually reading them. Hung above it was a mirror, and I stared at myself in it, hood back, exposing my youthful features.

My life lately had been a sequence of improbable disaster after improbable disaster—it left me wondering, was this what my life would be like from here on out? What about school? I hadn't particularly enjoyed school, mind you, but I was pretty sure that there were things left for me to learn.*

I stared into that reflection as the dinosaurs continued their fight behind me.

Then the me in the mirror walked away.

I gasped, jumping back, reaching into my pocket for one of my Lenses. A Librarian trap? But no . . . the mirror suddenly showed another place, a place like what I

---

* How was I going to properly write arrogant footnotes to everything if I didn't know everything there was to know?

thought I'd seen in the glass of the storefront on the street above.

White pillars, cobbled streets, statues and fountains . . .

Incarna, I thought. The kingdom from way, way back where the Smedry line—and the Talents—had begun. It was a bit like Greece, but with cooler clothing.*

In the mirror, Incarna was burning.

I stepped up to the mirror and raised my fingers to it. The glass was cool to the touch, but I felt as if it should burn me. The phantom version of me moved through the streets, and my view followed, showing me a ruined paradise. Flames flickered out of buildings that, made of stone, should definitely *not* have burned.

A shock of some sort made everything tremble, and a nearby building collapsed, spewing dust. The phantom passed, as if oblivious to the destruction.

I'm watching it, I realized. *The day Incarna fell*. Refugees had fled, some making it to Alexandria—where eventually my great-great, super-great-grandfather had died and been buried.

He'd blamed the Talents. Was that what had lurked inside me? The power to destroy cities? Continents? *Civilizations?*

---

* Their togas had spoilers and they wore sunglasses.

Why in the world did I feel like I wanted the thing back?

The Alcatraz in the mirror had grown more shadowy—almost smoky. It moved through the burning town, approaching a place where the buildings were actually *melting*. They broke apart, large sections turning molten red. Ahead, a brilliant light shot toward the sky.

I frowned, pressing against the glass. Did I . . . did I *recognize* that light from somewhere?

"Cousin?"

I jumped, spinning around to find Dif standing behind me, watching me with a cocked head. The dinosaurs continued their mock battle, screaming now with what seemed like pain—all the while throwing *furniture* at the *walls*.

"Wow," I said. "They're really getting into it."

"We all have a savage side to us," Dif said. "Some bury it more deeply than most. Why were you staring at that mirror?"

I spun back around, but the glass had reverted to normal, just showing my face. "I . . ." I said, then shook my head. "Do you know what kind of glass this is?"

"Aren't you the Oculator?"

Of course. Idiot. I pulled out my Oculator's Lenses and

looked at the mirror, but the glass gave off no glow. There wasn't anything special about it.

I tucked away the Lenses.

"Are you all right, Cousin?" Dif said. "I mean, I know we're supposed to be strange and kooky, but I hadn't realized that extended to making out with mirrors. . . ."

"I wasn't 'making out' with it."

Behind us, Douglas yelled something about a fort made of brassieres, something else about arresting silence, then let out a string of *Oh*s like he was singing in a boy band. Finally he collapsed to the floor.

"Dif," I said. "You're *sure* your Talent is still working?"

"It is," Dif said. "I used it outside, when we were first put into that group of Librarians."

So that *was* how he'd slipped away. "What happened? What did it do?"

Dif shrugged. "You tell me. You were looking right at me when I used it."

"I was?"

He nodded.

"I can't remember a thing."

"That's the Talent for you," Dif said. "So . . . when are you going to use yours? I'll be honest, I've wanted to see the Breaking Talent in action for quite some time."

I started, then realized we'd never explained it to him, not directly. "I broke the other Talents," I said, walking back through the stacks toward the dinosaurs.

"What, *really*?" he said, following.

"Yeah," I said. "Mine isn't working, and neither is Grandpa's, or Kaz's. I'm wondering if what I did was localized—like, maybe only the people who were nearby me lost their Talents, since yours is still working." I shook my head. "Once we get out of here, we'll need to contact the other Smedrys and see if their Talents are working or not."

Dif nodded, seeming stunned by this information. I stepped up to the dinosaurs. Douglas the T. rex lay on his back, little arms sticking straight up. "How was that?" he asked.

"Perfect," I said, picking up the sword I'd brought in. "I'll bet the Librarians are horrified. When we get back to them, hopefully they'll lead us where we want to go."

"Do we have to go back to them, Cousin?" Dif asked. "We could just continue on deeper into the Highbrary."

"We'd have no idea where we were going."

"Oh, I don't know about that," Dif said. "I think I'm getting a feel for this place. Besides, how complicated can it be? Librarians made it, and we all know they aren't the brightest of people!"

"Don't underestimate them," I said. "There's no reason to be foolhardy."

"Huh?" he asked, confused. "I never thought we *needed* a reason."

I helped Douglas to his feet—no small task, since even though he was a small T. rex, he still must have weighed like a gaglazillion pounds.*

"You're *sure* you don't want to slip out the back?" Dif asked, thumbing over his shoulder.

"Quite sure," I said, looking to Douglas. "Now," I said to him. "I'm afraid I'm going to have to ask you to bite your lip again. . . ."

---

* Bastille insisted I look this one up, so for the record, he only weighs 0.73 gaglazillion pounds.

Chapter

16

Yes, I mentioned Bastille in that last chapter.*

Presumably this removes some of the tension for you in this book. After all, if she's talking to me in the future when I am writing these books, then she obviously gets healed. Right?

Yup. Bastille is fine.

She's not the one who dies in this book.

I stepped out onto the rope bridge, carrying a sword covered in Douglas's blood. (And yes, he wasn't kidding:

---

* It was in a footnote. So if you don't look at them, you missed it. Like you're missing this one right now, which means I can say anything about you that I want, and you won't see it. But what's the fun in that?

A T. rex's bit lip can be really amazing in its blood-flow output.) Dif joined me as we silently crossed the gap.

Librarians clustered around the place where the bridge ended. They'd been creeping forward—the Dark Oculator at the very back—to see what was going on. I stopped in the center of the bridge and held up the bloody sword, causing a round of murmurs from the pile of Librarians.

Far beneath me, the fans went *wub, wub, wub.*

Then they went *wubwubwubwub.*

Finally they went something like: *WUBWUBWUBWUB-WUBWOWWE'REGOINGFASTNOWMATE!*

For some reason, the fans had chosen that moment to go into overdrive. This was an air intake for the ventilation system, meaning the fans drew in the air and pushed it throughout the entire Highbrary. And that meant I was suddenly in the middle of a vortex of wind, blowing down from above, trying to suck me off the bridge and into the fans.

I shouted in alarm and dropped the sword, grabbing the sides of the bridge and holding tight. Dif did the same, looking at me with a surprised expression.

Wait. I could see his expression. His hood had fallen back in the wind. Which meant . . . yes, mine had as well.

I looked toward the Librarians. They looked back.

Then the Dark Oculator screamed in terror and ran away back down the tunnel. The other Librarians followed, leaving behind a solitary figure who put her hands on her hips.

Dif and I pulled ourselves across the bridge as it swayed dangerously. Fortunately we made it across, though just as we stepped off, the bridge pitched from side to side, then finally ripped apart.

I gulped as I watched the wooden planks get sucked down into the vortex. I glanced at Dif, who looked nonplussed.* Something was *definitely* wrong with those fans.

Now that we were out of the wind tunnel directly above the fans, the air wasn't being pulled as much. Still, we walked down the hallway to get away from the noise.

"You know," my mother said, looking in the direction the Librarians had fled, "that was completely unfair."

"Huh?"

"Why are they afraid of *you*?" she said, folding her arms and tapping her foot. "Do you know how hard I tried to cultivate a fearsome reputation? They don't care about me, but they run away from a teenage kid with a bad haircut? Bother."

---

* Which, by the way, is kind of a stupid word. What does it mean to be plussed anyway? Sounds like something mathematical.

"You're a terrible mother. You realize that, don't you?"

"I'll bake you cookies or something to make up for it," Shasta said. She hesitated. "That's a thing mothers do, right?"

"You don't know?"

"Never got around to studying for the job," Shasta said. "Honestly, you'd think they'd give us an instruction manuel* or something."

Well, regardless, this plan hadn't turned out. Not only had I lost my cool bloody sword, the Librarians had run away.

"Well, now what?" I asked as we stopped in the tunnel.

"Hmm?" Shasta asked.

"That Dark Oculator was going to lead us to the Forgotten Language texts."

"Why would she do that?" Dif asked.

"She thought I was serving the Scrivener," I explained. "I told her I'd been sent by him."

Dif started. "What?"

"Yeah," I said. "She wanted to test that I was as powerful as I claimed, so she sent me to kill the monster."

"Dinosaurs," Shasta said dismissively. "I can't believe

---

* ¡Hola!

that nobody noticed. Hasn't anyone in here heard a T. rex throw a tantrum before?"

Drat. I'd been hoping she'd think I'd done something incredible. "Well, the Dark Oculator is gone, so she can't lead us to the Forgotten Language archive. Now we'll have to start all over."

"Yes," Shasta said. "We could do that. Or we could use this." She held up a small, mobile-phone-like device.

"Is that—"

"The Dark Oculator's authenticator?" Shasta said. "Yes."

"And you—"

"Picked her pocket," Shasta said. "What? You thought I was just lounging out here composing an epic ballad or something? Thank you for the distraction, by the way."

"Great. Let's turn it on!"

Mother tucked it into her pocket.

"Wait! What are you doing?"

"Let's go over those rules again," she said, looking me in the eyes.

"They aren't negotiable."

"Really? That's too bad." She started to walk away.

I grabbed her by the arm. "You turn that thing on."

"Or *what*, Alcatraz? Are you willing to hurt me to get what you want? Do you think you could actually manage it if you decided to try?"

I looked to Dif, who shrugged, seeming to say, "I told you we should have snuck away on our own."

I looked back to my mother, grinding my teeth. "What do you want?"

"When we find your father," she said. "You may talk to him. You may try to get him to see some sense. But if he doesn't listen, *I* get to deal with him. In any way necessary."

"No. We can't—"

"What do you think we're doing here, boy?" she snapped. "Are we playing games? Have you been with that fool of a grandfather of yours so long you've lost the ability to see the world as it *has* to be?"

I stepped back, shocked by her outburst.

"We," she shouted, "are going to stop him. That's what we came to do. Even if it rips us up inside, we are going to *stop him*. DO YOU UNDERSTAND?"

"I . . ."

Did I?

Why else had we come? What steps *was* I willing to take?

"As long as I get to talk to him first," I said, reluctant. "You don't take any . . . steps until I am done and give you the go-ahead."

"Fine," Mother said. "But I only concede because I

hope, against my better judgment, that he'll listen to you when he never listened to me."

Mother clicked something on the authenticator, and a spray of light rose from it, projecting a three-dimensional set of glowing red gridlines into the air. It showed all of the passageways, archives, and chambers of the High-brary. Projected like this, it looked a lot like an anthill with tons of tunnels and burrows.

I located where we'd entered—a place near the middle of the main chamber, easily recognized because of the tall, spindly tower topped by an altar.*

From there, I followed our trail on the map to locate the fan chamber. There were several of them marked on the map—were all the fans blowing this hard? Even standing a distance away from it, the air current was noticeably strong.

This place was enormous. I squinted, reading notation after notation in the air. How long would we be safe just standing here? What if—

"There," Dif said, pointing at a notation. "Forgotten Language texts. Mauve-level authenticator required."

---

* Yes, I said altar. What did you think that stack of books atop it was? An altar. Made from old encyclopedias. No joke here. This paragraph was surprisingly hard for me to write; I'm going to take a break and eat a fish stick to wash the taste out of my mouth.

"And . . . what do we have?" I asked.

"Gamboge," Mother said.

"Which is . . . ?"

"High enough to get us in," she said.

I nodded in relief, memorizing the path between our location and the archive. We'd have to return to the main chamber, then head down a different set of tunnels. It was practically on *top* of another wind tunnel.

"Let's go," Mother said, moving to turn off the authenticator.

I stopped her, raising my hand, tracing the path again. I'd noticed something else on that map. It was practically on the way—

Suddenly the authenticator flashed brilliantly, the projected image growing much brighter. I backed away. Had I done that to it somehow? But I wasn't even *touching* it.

Mother flipped it off, looking annoyed. "It's hot to the touch," she complained, stuffing it back in her pocket. "What did you do?"

"Nothing!" I said. But there wasn't time to protest my innocence—I had a plan. Much like the old plan.

But with a quick diversion.

I took off running. Shasta grumbled and fell in behind me, Dif at the back. We emerged into the main cavern, with its sweeping rock bridges and hundreds of archive huts. A gaping hole in the ceiling spilled light down in a golden column near the center. The sound of gunfire popped in the distance—Himalaya's team was still fighting, thankfully.

We turned right. The Librarians in the main cavern were all abuzz, scurrying about, shouting. Something had sent them into a panic, it seemed. Most had suffered the exploding ceiling and the subsequent invasion with merely passing interest. Why would they suddenly be concerned?

Well, at least I didn't feel out of place breaking into a jog. Perhaps that would help us look busy, so nobody else would conscript us into a monster-slaying team.*

My mother pulled up alongside me as we jogged. "What's going on?"

"I have no idea." I fished in my robe pocket, bringing out the phone. It felt strange to be using something so ordinary, but there it was. It had only three numbers saved; I dialed the most recent one.

It rang, then Himalaya answered. "Yeah?" she said, sounding out of breath.

---

* Never thought I'd see that as a bad thing.

"Did you guys do something?" I asked.

"Other than get forced to the second floor of our building?" she said. I heard gunfire over her line. "This isn't going well, Alcatraz. They're going to overwhelm us soon."

"Understood," I said. "You guys should get out of there. I don't think we need you as a distraction any longer."

"Yeah," Himalaya said. "About that . . ."

I felt a chill.

"They dropped a Librarian task force onto the roof of the building where we're holed up," Himalaya said. "And they set up *sharpshooters* on the next building over. There's no way we're going to be able to use the grappling lines to climb to the surface. I was hoping you'd have some kind of plan to get us out. We're pinned down in here."

Shattering Glass.

"That distraction with the wind was helpful though," Himalaya added.

"The wind?" I said.

"Yeah," Himalaya said. "The ventilation is blowing into the archive at a furious rate, enough to knock over some of the shelves near the air duct in our building. It's scattering carefully catalogued piles of information in a completely casual, careless, and unorganized way. . . ."

I could hear her twitch over the line.

"You don't need to reorganize it all right now, Himalaya," I said, brushing past a group of anxious Librarians who were heading toward an archive where—inside—I could see a little mini vortex spinning sheets of paper in the air. Well, at least now I knew why they were acting so crazy.

"I know, I know," she said. "But it's so *messy*. Anyway, it's distracting to my people, but just as bad for the Librarians outside. The one reason we're still alive is because groups of enemies keep breaking off to go help clean one archive or another."

"At least that's something," I said.

"Alcatraz," Himalaya said softly. "There's one more thing. I touched a piece of Shielder's Glass here; we brought it along for cover, but it ran out of brightsand quickly. Alcatraz . . . when I touched it . . . it started glowing."

I felt cold.

"You're not an Oculator."

"No, never have been. Folsom isn't one either. But he can make the glass glow too. What does it mean?"

It meant I had no idea what was going on. It wasn't only me and Grandpa, it seemed, who were making glass act crazy. The effect was multiplied in us, but if it was happening to Himalaya and Folsom too . . .

"Alcatraz, please," she said. "I have to get back to the fighting. But if you can do something to help us out, we'd really appreciate it."

More people relying on me. I felt a knot in the bottom of my stomach as Himalaya hung up. The Free Kingdoms Air Guard had come, the Librarian resistance, even Charles and his friends, all because they'd believed in my speech. I was the face of this rebellion, improvised though it was.

How in the world was I going to save them? Most days it felt like I could barely save myself.

We reached the tunnel that would lead to the Forgotten Language archive, and turned into it. Once again our only light became that of skull-shaped lamps on the walls. This corridor felt quiet, almost solemn, compared to the chaos outside.

"The Scrivener," I said, shoving the phone back into my pocket and looking toward my mother. "That Dark Oculator confirmed to me that someone is using that name. Do you know what he looks like? Maybe we can confirm if this is Biblioden returned, or just someone using the title."

"That will be tough," my mother said. "We don't even have pictures of him—not that the Librarian high-ups show off. But . . . Alcatraz, I doubt any other Librarian would claim that title. We have to confront the possibility that Biblioden found a way to bring himself back to life. Either that or he was never actually dead in the first place."

I'd like to pause here and say something clever.

I'd like to, but I can't because I'm not really feeling clever at the moment. So instead I'm going to include the mating call of the wooly sea sloth:

"Hey, wanna grab a pizza?"

Ah, such magnificent animals.

We reached an intersection in our tunnel. The wind was blowing more strongly from the left fork, and that's the direction my mother turned. The direction of the archive we wanted.

I, however, turned right.

"Alcatraz?" my mother called, stopping at the intersection, though Dif followed me immediately. Finally I heard her footfalls racing after me down the corridor.

From my memory of the map, I only needed to count down four rooms in this tunnel to get where I wanted to go. When I arrived, I was disappointed to find a locked steel door blocking the entrance. Fortunately, when my mother drew close, a light on the side of the door turned green. The authenticator had enough clearance to get us in.

"What is this?" Dif asked.

"Chemicals lab and medical storage?" my mother asked, reading the words—etched into the stone in a cryptic language I couldn't decipher—above the entrance. "Why have you come here?"

I placed my hand on the door. "Because," I said, "I have a friend in a Librarian-induced coma, and this is *precisely* the sort of place they'd keep the cure."

Chapter

17

I can't drive a car. But if I *could* drive a car, and if this book were a car, my foot would be on the gas pedal and we'd be going about 200 miles an hour right now.

I've thought quite a bit about these last chapters of my autobiography. You are now approaching the end of the *fifth* book, the last book. You've dedicated hours upon hours of your life studying my exploits. It's all been pointing at this.

I want you to understand the gravity of this moment; I *need* you to realize exactly how solemn all this is. And so, I'm going to do something I've never done before. Something incredible, something dangerous, and something completely unexpected.

I'm going to let you skip ahead.

Yes, I know. In every book so far, I've forbidden you from looking ahead. I've mocked and derided those who do so. I told you to never, never, *never* look ahead in a book.

And now I'm letting you. That's how important this ending is. That's how dangerous all this is.

We have to do it in a controlled way though. At the end of this introduction, I am giving you formal permission to look ahead to Chapter Twenty and read the first two paragraphs on page 273.

Now, make sure you read *only* the first two paragraphs, and of *only* that chapter. No peeking at anything else. Just those two paragraphs.

Read them out loud.

I inched open the door into the chemical storage facility and got a faceful of wind; the air vents inside were blowing full force. This chamber was all smooth metal surfaces, distinctly different from the organic "rocky cavern" feel of the rest of the Highbrary. A pair of Librarians moved inside, stacking a set of glass tubes on a rack. They wore white robes instead of black, and spoke in hushed whispers.

"I'm telling you, I *saw* it," one of them was saying. "I was on the expedition to Alexandria; I know what they look like. I don't know why those spirits are making their way here, but they are."

I pulled back, letting Dif and my mother peek through

the crack. "We'll have to wait until those Librarians are gone," I whispered to the two of them.

"No time," my mother said.

She stood up and shoved her way into the room. I stifled a yelp of annoyance and fished for my Shame-filler's Lens. But I didn't dare use that on people. Not even Librarians. I—

"You two!" my mother barked. "We have wounded in the main hall."

The two Librarian scientists—a man and a woman—spun about, took in Mother's black robe, then glanced at the light on the wall indicating that she was allowed into the room.

"Wounded?" the male Librarian scientist asked. "Why would there be wounded?"

"Haven't you been paying attention?" Mother snapped. "Useless fools! Rebels have broken into the Highbrary."

"Did they cause the wind?" the other scientist asked, pointing toward a stack of papers they'd had to weigh down with beakers full of water.

"Obviously," Mother said. "They also brought some of our own weapons, stolen from the battlefield in Mokia, and are using them to knock our troops unconscious. I need the cure, stat."

"Stat?" the woman asked.

"It's Latin," my mother said. "It means I'll rip out your tongues if you don't obey *RIGHT NOW*."

They obeyed, rushing to a cabinet and unlocking it. My mother folded her arms as I joined her; then she cocked an eyebrow at me. I might not have thought highly of her parenting skills, but I did have to admit that she had an enviable ability to get her way. People tended to do what she said, if only because her presence was so loathsome they wanted to be free of her as soon as possible.

The female scientist came back with a tiny vial, smaller than a perfume sampler. My mother looked at it, skeptical.

"We'll need way more than one vial," I said.

"No you won't," the woman said, unscrewing the lid. "This stuff is super concentrated. You'd be surprised at how much a few drops can do. We merely have to hold it up beneath the subject's nose, and once they smell the fumes they'll awaken."

The vial let out a distinctive scent of cinnamon. It seemed safe to breathe. My mother looked to me, and I nodded. It would at least be enough for Bastille.

"We'll take it," my mother said, reaching for the vial.

"We're not allowed to let level-eight superchemicals out of our sight," the woman said, putting the lid back on.

My mother glared at her, but the scientist remained firm.

"Fine," my mother snapped. "Take it to the central sanctum, near the altar. Administer it to any who have fallen."

"Uh . . ." the woman said, shuffling. "Is that where everyone is fighting . . . ?"

"That's what I said."

"But I'm a scientist."

"Don't worry," my mother said. "You can take your colleague. I'm certain the two of you will be safe together."

After a short staring match, the woman wilted, then nodded. The two scientists left, scuttling away before my mother's glare like they'd been caught eating apples in Eden.

I pushed the door shut behind them, then hurried to the cabinet where they'd gotten out the vial. It was locked. I pried at it, cursing softly. The whole thing was metal. I'd need a crowbar to get in.

"This is a waste of our time," Mother said, folding her arms.

"My friends," I muttered, "are counting on me."

"Your friends are not as important as the fate of the world."

"I've kind of got to agree," Dif said. "As awesomely yet irresponsibly impulsive as this was, Cousin, we can't spend much time here."

"Just a minute," I said, grabbing a screwdriver off a nearby table, then trying to use it to pry the medicine case open.

This was ridiculous. Here I was, trying to break something. And failing. How often had *that* happened in my life? True, my Talent had occasionally broken everything except the item I wanted, but during these last few months with my family, I'd learned control. I'd stopped breaking things by accident. I'd channeled my powers, as Grandpa had taught.

And now . . . nothing. It was alarming how powerless I suddenly felt, unable to get through that little sheet of metal and its stupid lock. After a few minutes of fruitless struggling, feeling my mother's and Dif's eyes on me, I slammed the screwdriver down on the metal desk next to me with a resonant *bang*.

If there was one thing I was supposed to be able to do, it was break things! It was like a fundamental part of me was missing. Was this how Grandpa and the others felt? I'd been somewhat enjoying the loss of my Talent—it hadn't been that long ago that I'd viewed it as a curse, rather than a super power.

I turned to look at the others, to beg for help getting the cabinet open, and I caught my reflection in a nearby glass case. It was watching me, and it didn't move when I did.

"You're it, aren't you?" I asked the reflection. "The Talent?"

"Alcatraz?" my mother asked.

I ignored her, looking into my own eyes in the glass. The figure shook its head.

I jumped. I was expecting that, but I still jumped.

"What are you, then?" I demanded.

The figure mouthed something. *I'm you.*

"You broke things," I said. "You broke *everything*. That wasn't me. I didn't *want* to."

Didn't you? the figure asked. *You didn't want to drive them away? You didn't want to be alone?*

"I . . ."

What am I to you? the figure mouthed. I could almost hear it. *Something to be controlled, bottled in, used? Then ignored?*

"Why did you do this?" I asked, stepping up to the glass. "Why did you let me save Mokia, then *leave*?"

Maybe, the figure mouthed, *I was tired of being blamed for things that are not my fault.*

I stared at the glass, and found tears leaking from the corners of my eyes. My mother stepped up to me, hesitant, as if she were approaching a wild animal. She touched me on the arm. "Alcatraz? Are you all right?"

"No," I snapped, turning from her to the cabinet. I

placed my hands on the metal and tried to summon the Talent. I reached for it, *strained* for it.

I was so close. Just another inch . . .

It refused.

But my robe did start talking to me again.

"I can't believe I let my hood fall down right at the wrong moment!" it cried. "I ruined everything!"

And if this seems like too many talking inanimate objects for you, might I kindly remind you that you're the one talking to a book.*

The Shamefiller's Lens. I cursed, digging it out of my pocket, but the thing was brutally hot to the touch. It singed my fingers and I dropped it. It bounced to a rest on the floor and released a distinctive beam of light straight upward.

"Man, I'm a terrible ceiling. . . ."

I can't believe that the last thing I said to Bastille was a complaint that she was supposed to protect me, a piece of me thought. *I'm so ashamed. . . .*

Uh-oh.

"Out!" I screamed at the others, then grabbed the screwdriver and ducked down, using it to tilt the Lens up toward the cabinet.

------

* You are reading this out loud, aren't you? I mean, I'm sure I've told you to do that with these books at some point.

"Wow," the cabinet said, "I can't believe I slammed on that cute scientist's fingers. It was absolutely the wrong moment too. There we were, the two of us, alone in here and, and, I can't take it!"

No. I couldn't destroy the cabinet. That would break the vials. Instead, I tipped the Lens toward the wall nearby. It was a long shot too, but I felt better about it.

"I'm the worst wall ever," the wall said. "All I do is stare at the other walls. Do they see the dirty specks on me? Is that why they won't speak to me? Oh!"

I failed her, I thought. *I failed everyone. . . .*

A section of the wall exploded as my screwdriver head melted. As I'd hoped, the wall ripping apart made the metal cabinet fall free. I managed to catch it, and the back was open. From within I grabbed a large bottle of liquid the same shade as the little vial the scientist had shown us.

"I'm the worst floor ever."

"What an *awful* table I am!"

I ruined everything, I thought. *I'm so terrible at all of this, I could just explode. . . .*

I dove for the doorway, cradling the bottle as things inside the room began to burst in showers of sparks. The ceiling, the tables, the walls. Their blasts created a thundering cacophony.

But I survived.

Though a lingering sense of shame haunted me, I'd gotten far enough away. I was left with the image of a large column of light consuming everything in the room.

"What," my mother said, "was *that*?"

"Lenses are acting kind of weird around me," I said, struggling to my feet.

"That's what you call '*weird*'?" she demanded as the entire room collapsed upon itself.

Dazed, I fished in my pocket. I'd dropped the Truth-finder's Lens into the fans, so all I had left now were my standard Oculator's Lenses and my Courier's Lenses. Well, those and the Shaper's Lens my grandfather had given me.

"Come on," I said, holding the large bottle of antidote. "Let's move."

I got no complaint from the others, and Dif gave me a thumbs-up. He apparently considered what I'd just done to be properly "kooky" and "unexpected." I pulled out the Courier's Lenses and put them on as we ran down the hallway. "Grandpa?" I said, activating them. I couldn't worry about the fact that they'd make me glow; hopefully everyone would assume I was a Dark Oculator.

NO NEED TO YELL, LAD! Grandpa's voice screamed back at me.

"I'm not yelling, you are."

MUST BE THE WAY WE'RE SUDDENLY SUPER-CHARGING LENSES.

"I suppose," I said, lagging behind Shasta and Dif. That burst of shamefilling had really taken a lot out of me. "We found where they're keeping the Forgotten Language texts, and are on our way there right now."

ROUSING ROWLINGS! I'M ON MY WAY TOO! YOU FOUND AN AUTHENTICATOR?

"Both that and the antidote for the Mokians. I took our authenticator off a Dark Oculator. You?"

TRICKED IT OUT OF ONE OF THE LIBRARIANS WHO OPERATE THE VENTILATION SYSTEMS IN HERE. RIGHT BEFORE JAMMING THE THINGS ON FULL SPEED.

"That was *you*?" I asked.

FIGURED IT WOULD MESS EVERYTHING UP IN HERE. LIBRARIANS CAN NEVER THINK STRAIGHT IF THEIR BOOKS ARE OUT OF ORDER.

I decided not to mention how the fans had nearly messed *me* up as well. "So that's your plan to destroy the place? Wind tunnels?"

WELL, THAT, Grandpa said, *AND ENGAGING THE HIGHBRARY'S SELF-DESTRUCT MECHANISM.*

I stopped in place. "The *what*?"

DON'T SHOUT, PLEASE, LAD! Grandpa said, but

chuckled. *THE SELF-DESTRUCT MECHANISM. EVIL SOCIETIES CAN NEVER RESIST PUTTING THE SILLY THINGS IN THEIR BASES.*

"But . . ." I said.

DON'T WORRY, Grandpa replied. *THEY'LL GET IT DISARMED BEFORE IT GOES OFF. I'VE NEVER YET BEEN ABLE TO GET ONE OF THE BLASTED THINGS TO ACTUALLY BLOW UP, BUT IT WILL SEND THE HIGH-LEVEL LIBRARIANS INTO A PANIC, MAYBE KEEP THEM OFF OUR BACKS. I'LL MEET YOU AT THE FORGOTTEN LANGUAGE ARCHIVE.*

I nodded. Ahead, my mother had stopped in the wide tunnel, looking back at me insistently. The wind was pretty strong here. Not "blow you over" strong, but maybe "blow over your baby brother" strong.

I continued forward, feeling drained. Perhaps it was the lingering effect of the Shamefiller's Lens, but I had a sudden, almost overpowering feeling that this was all going to end like it had in Mokia. Maybe we'd stop my father, but what about saving my friends? What about Himalaya and Folsom, and all the people fighting in ships above the city? What good was it to "win" if everyone I cared about ended up dying for that victory?

I dug out the phone and dialed Kaz.

"Al!" he said, picking up the phone. I could hear

explosions on the other end of the line. "Please tell me you're almost done in there."

"Battle's going poorly?"

"You could say that," Kaz said, then cursed. He didn't speak for a few seconds. "That was close. We're going to need to pull out soon. And Al, something strange is going on."

"Glass is acting oddly around you?"

"Yeah! How'd you guess? When I push buttons on the glass control panel, it lights them *all* up. It's nearly gotten me killed. I have to steer with the most delicate touch. I don't know how long I can keep this up before something goes very wrong."

"Okay," I said, "I want you to pull out. But I need you to do something crazy first."

"How crazy?"

"Way crazy."

"I'm sold. What is it?"

"I need you to dive down the hole we made into the Highbrary," I said. "Himalaya and Folsom are in here with a team of soldiers, and they're trapped. I want you to land *Penguinator*, pick them up, then escape."

"You're right," he said. "That *is* crazy. I'll do it."

"Once they're aboard, retreat."

"And you?"

"I've got another way out," I lied.

I didn't want more people dying because of the stupid things I'd said to the monarchs. Grandpa, Dif, and I would have to find our own way out. Smedrys always escaped from these kinds of scrapes, right?

"Any news on bringing the Talents back?" Kaz asked.

"Not yet."

"Pity. I keep feeling like I can *almost* get my Talent working. . . ." He signed off, and I texted him Himalaya's number, then sent a text to Himalaya too, telling her to prepare for Kaz's arrival. Using technology again was pretty weird; I kept expecting the phone to melt in my fingers or talk back to me or something.

My mother and Dif slowed ahead of me. Could they power glass too? I wanted to test the theory, but I dithered, wondering what would happen if I gave Mother this information.

The authenticator, I thought. *It was going haywire in her hands, without me touching it. She might be interfering with the glass that runs it.*

More questions. Feeling exhausted and confused, I joined the other two at a set of metal doors. The lights on the sides of the entrance glowed green. We could enter.

If we really wanted to. That was questionable, since as the doors opened, I could see that most of the floor inside was missing.

Yes, *missing.* The only thing resembling a floor was the long walkway leading from our doorway to a platform in the center of the room. That platform had a hut on it, like the archives out in the main chamber. I could see bookshelves within.

Other than that, the room was a pit. A familiar *wub-wub-wub* came from below. There was no ceiling, just a long dark opening like there had been in the other ventilation shaft. Wind rushed from the open tunnel above, getting sucked downward by those fans to be pushed throughout the entire Highbrary.

"Fans," I said. "They built the Forgotten Language archive above a pit of doom?"

"Librarians," my mother said, "share more with Smedrys than either would like to admit. Both will bend over backward to accommodate sheer dramatic effect."

I shivered, but there was nothing to do but cross that walkway. At least it looked more sturdy than the rope bridge had been. My mother led, with me next, and Dif in the rear. There weren't any handrails, and though the walkway was a good four or five feet wide, I felt like it was a tightrope—wind tossing my hair and clothing, each step threatening to topple me down into those fan blades.

Never was I so happy to enter a library as I was to step off that walkway and into the room of that little hut, where—fortunately—the wind was far less severe. The place seemed empty of people. It was lit by electric lights on the walls and stocked with hundreds of texts in the Forgotten Language, many of which were scrolls.

"Empty," Dif said, hands on his hips. "Weren't we supposed to find your father here?"

"Oh, he's here," I said.

"Where?" my mother asked.

"He has Disguiser's Lenses on."

"Haven't you been paying attention?" my mother demanded. "The Highbrary has precautions in place against things like that. Anyone using Lenses to imitate someone else will glow."

"Oh, I know," I said. "Attica is counting on that, as it helps the disguise. Isn't that right, Father?"

Something moved beside a bookcase, coming out from a hiding place. A ghostly figure, glowing, spectral clothing hanging in tatters. It was wearing a monocle.

One of the undead Curators, the Librarians who haunted Alexandria. Or someone dressed like one.

"How did you guess?" the ghost said, using my father's voice.

Chapter

18

The Librarians are afraid of a ghost," I said to him. "Specifically one of the Alexandrian types. And who better to imitate one of them than the only man who joined their ranks, then escaped? Besides, if Librarian defenses are going to make you glow, why not incorporate that into your disguise?" I shrugged. Made sense to me.

"Well done," my father said, the ghostly image vanishing—replaced by his normal form. Attica Smedry was a tall, handsome man with too much smile to him. He wore a pair of Lenses and had on a stylish Free Kingdoms outfit that—in my opinion—looked a lot like pajamas.

When my father and I had been together in Nalhalla, he'd been quick to endear himself to everyone he considered important.

I hadn't been included.

Perhaps that's the fable of these books. You, reader, may have a beef* with your parents, but chances are they're not anywhere *near* as bad as mine. At least your mother doesn't belong to an evil cult that has conquered half the world, and at least your father isn't inadvertently trying to destroy the other half.

"It . . . is a good disguise, Attica," my mother said. "Librarians who saw it would wonder, 'Why is one of the Curators of Alexandria floating around our halls?' instead of wondering if you're a spy. They spent their time trying to solve the wrong puzzle. By standing out, your true motives became invisible. It's brilliant, as usual."

"Thank you," my father said.

Mother reached into the pocket of her jacket and took out a handgun.

"Mother!" I cried out. "The rules! Your promise!"

"Promises mean nothing," she said, "when the fate of a planet is on the line."

"This is an old argument, Shasta," my father said, raising his hands to the sides. "One I'm bored of hearing. It won't destroy the world; it will simply destroy the Librarians."

---

* Cake?

"Smedry Talents?" she said. "In the hands of everyone?"

"Equality," my father said.

"Fame for you."

"Don't be petty," my father snapped. "This *will* break Biblioden's control. The Librarians want to pretend the world is 'normal' and 'straightforward'? They want to ignore the Free Kingdoms? Well, let them ignore *this*. A Talent for every person!"

"Insanity."

"Inevitability," he said. "You can't stop it, not even if you kill me. Someone will crack this eventually. It might as well be me."

"It always comes back to your ego," she said, raising the gun. I felt a spike of alarm. "Everything *always* comes down to that."

My father met her eyes. "He's returned, you know."

My mother didn't speak.

"Biblioden," my father said. "He has reappeared. I suspect he knew his plots needed centuries to grow, and so he found a way to put himself to sleep and wait, giving his kingdom time to expand. Now that the victory is within his grasp—the end of the Free Kingdoms—he has returned to deliver the killing blow. Well, *I'll* give the people a weapon to fight against him. Let's see how the

Librarians do when every person they try to dominate has the Breaking Talent!"

"You're mad," my mother whispered. Though she held the gun steady, I could see a tear on her cheek.

"Mother!" I repeated. *"Mother!"*

She glanced at me.

"You promised," I said. "I talk to him first."

"He won't change, Alcatraz. He *never* changes."

"But do you really want to pull that trigger without knowing?" I asked. "Without giving him one more chance?"

My mother hesitated, then sighed and lowered her gun.

A beam of light shot from my father's right eye and smashed into her, tossing her backward. She hit the floor, unconscious, and the gun skidded from her fingers toward the doorway.

"Mother!" I screamed, rushing to her side.

"Oh, don't worry," my father said, chuckling. "It's only a Concussor's Lens. She'll wake up with a headache in a few hours, knowing I bested her yet again. She's used to that by now, I do suspect."

I turned my mother onto her back. Indeed she was breathing, but the side of her face was bright red, as if she'd been hit really hard.

"Hmmm," my father said. "The Lens is acting up

again. I didn't realize I'd put so much power through it. Well, good job getting her to put down the gun, my boy! That was some solid teamwork there."

Now I was "my boy"?

"Dif," I said. "Go out in front of the hut here and watch for Grandfather. He said he was coming. Give me warning if Librarians come instead."

"Sure thing," Dif said, slipping out of the hut's front.

My father continued chuckling to himself as he removed a stack of hidden notebooks from behind a bookshelf. "Shasta *really* should have guessed that I was wearing two different Lenses," he said. "Disguiser's Lens in one eye, Concussor's in the other. One of the oldest tricks in the book, even if it *is* challenging to wear two different Lenses at once."

I reluctantly left Shasta on the ground. She was a bad mother, but not a bad person—at least she was trying to do what was right. I didn't have the same confidence about my father.

"Here, my boy, let me show you what I've discovered!" Attica sat down at a table, swapping his Lenses for a different pair. I recognized these new ones. Translator's Lenses. Those were the first type of Lenses I'd ever owned—at least, if you counted the bag of sand that arrived for me on my birthday.

"We really *can* do this," my father said, flipping through his notes, pushing aside a stack of Forgotten Language texts. To my unaided eyes, they just looked like scribbles on a page—and not even in a "this is a language I don't know" way. It resembled the squiggles and loops a toddler might draw.

"Father, I'm not convinced we want to give everyone Talents," I said, looking over his shoulder at his notes. "What if Mother's right? What if this will cause a disaster?"

"Nonsense," Father said. "Son, you have to understand. Your mother is a *Librarian*. In her heart she's terrified of change—not to mention frightened of the idea of common people being outside her control. I mean, look what she did to you during your youth."

And you were any better? I thought. At least she'd kept an eye on me. Who knows where Attica had been for most of that time?

"What I've discovered here is *revolutionary*," my father said. "It changes everything."

"What do you mean?" I needed to get him talking, to stall long enough for Grandfather to arrive. I felt completely incapable when dealing with my father, but Grandpa . . . he'd know what to do.

"It's all here," my father said, spreading out his hands.

"The history of the Incarna. How they went about bringing Smedry Talents into the world."

"Those Talents destroyed them," I said, shivering.

"No, they didn't." Attica turned to me, eyes twinkling. He looked like his father at that moment. "That's
the secret, Son. That's what everyone's been wrong about.
The Talents *weren't* responsible for the destruction of
Incarna."

"Alcatraz the First thought they were," I said. "He left a
warning about the Breaking Talent. He called it . . . what,
the 'Bane of Incarna'?"

"Alcatraz the First was a fool," my father said with a
dismissive wave of his hand. "He hated the Talent, said
it had betrayed him. These records claim that it was not
because his Talent destroyed his people—they insist his
anger was because his Talent failed to *save* his people."

"Failed to . . . Huh?"

"I'm not sure what it means," my father said, voice
growing softer as he flipped through his notes. "But
these books are clear. The Talents were created to *stop* the
destruction of Incarna, after the place was already in danger. I don't know how they were supposed to help. But I do
know that they didn't destroy the Incarna—what really
brought the civilization down was power. Energy."

He opened to a page and tapped it with the back of his

fingers before continuing. "Energy drives the world, Son. Oil, coal, brightsand. The Incarna invented all kinds of glass, but their means of powering these discoveries was limited. Brightsand was so hard for them to mine. Oculators were extremely rare, and could only use specific, specialized types of Lenses. They wanted something else, something more. And they found it. A source of power so vast, it could charge all the glass they wanted it to."

"What was it?" I asked, growing genuinely interested.

"Something dangerous," my father whispered. "I don't know yet what it was. But they were determined to use it. They found it unfair that there were so few Oculators. They all wanted to be like Oculators and have glass to use however they wanted. But this power they discovered, they couldn't control it. It was too much for them."

And suddenly I understood.

The destruction of Incarna.

The column of light.

The reason I could power glass with a touch.

And the truth behind the Talents. The reason they acted out so much, when we didn't want them to.

"It's us," I whispered. "We're the power source."

"What's that?" my father said.

"They did something to our family line," I said.

The pillar of light in my vision—it was like the column of destruction from a Firebringer's Lens.

"They created us," I said, "to power their glass and give their culture energy. They created us too strong though, and glass started to go crazy around us. Like it's doing now. They made us all Oculators—no, not just Oculators, but some type of super-Oculators, capable of charging all kinds of glass."

"Interesting," my father said.

"Most of the Talents mimic the powers of Lenses," I said. "What if the Talents are an outgrowth of what happened when the Incarna created us? Or . . . no, Father, you said they were intended to help somehow. Perhaps they bestowed the Talents as a way to stop the destruction. A way to funnel off the energy.

"That makes sense. . . . It's starting to happen to Kaz and Himalaya too. It's stronger in Grandpa, me, and you because we're also Oculators. Naturally born ones, magnifying the power the Incarna gave us. Alcatraz the First was one too. And now that the Talents are gone, the power source has nowhere to go. It's building up, and releasing when we touch glass—any of us. But how did they give us the Talents in the first place?"

"Interesting," my father said.

I looked at him. He wasn't even paying attention to me!

He was reading another page, nodding absently, but didn't seem to have heard what I'd told him.

"Father, how did the Incarna give us the Talents?"

"Hmm?"

"The *Talents*," I said. "How did the Incarna bring them to us?"

"Oh, well, it has to do with something they called the 'dark powers.' I think I can replicate what they did, though I'll need to go to the Worldspire. It's connected to every living being, you see, and so if I perform the ceremony correctly, I can use that connection to send the Talents to the world. Perfect, I'd say. So elegant."

"The . . . dark powers. That term doesn't bother you?"

"Should it?" he asked absently.

I stepped back. Ignoring me, as always. I sighed, moving to go wait for Grandfather, but then I stopped.

There was something I needed to know. I fished in my pocket and brought out my Shaper's Lens. It was warm to the touch; I was powering it without wanting to. We *were* the energy source the Incarna had created, somehow. Always before, the Talents had been there to take our excess energy and do something with it, like a drainage pipe used to shunt away excess rainfall.

I held up the Lens, looking at my father. Grandpa had

warned me about this, had said it could give me too much information. Unfair information.

I used it anyway, and I started to glow.

Through it I saw what my father wanted most in life. I saw him standing atop a pillar, surrounded by a sea of people looking at him with adoring eyes. Some shouted to him with excitement; others tossed gifts. He was idolized, loved by all.

That was exactly what I'd expected. But in the vision, *I* stood at his right, and Shasta stood at his left. Sure, it was an idealized version of each of us—I was more like a kid from an old '50s television show, with overalls and freckles. Mom wore a cheery dress and was smiling sweetly. But we were there.

I pulled the Lens away. Somehow it would have all been easier if his version of a perfect world hadn't included us. He *did* want a family. He wanted me, at least kind of.

"Here, Alcatraz, come look at this," my father said. "You've got to read what Plato said about his visit to the Incarna. It's remarkable."

I remained in place. Suddenly I wished I'd never been given this Shaper's Lens. What good was it doing me? I shoved it into my pocket. "Father," I said, "we don't know what effect the Talents will have on ordinary people."

"What's that?"

"*Listen* to me for once," I said, taking him by the arm. "Our family line is the power source. *We* are what the Incarna created. The Talents work because we power them. So what will it do to common people to gain them?"

"We . . . are the power source. . . ." My father's eyes opened wide. "Why yes, of *course*."

"We can't proceed," I said, "until we know what the Talents will do to ordinary people. We have to learn from what our ancestors did. We can study, but we can't just barrel into this without thinking! Like . . . like . . ."

Like a Smedry?

My father's face fell. He yanked his arm out of my grip. "You sound like *her*. Well, you'll both see sense once I'm done. You'll admit that this was an incredible discovery."

There really was no changing him, was there?

"Son?" a voice asked.

Finally. I turned with relief as Grandpa Smedry and Draulin entered, Dif walking beside them.

"So," Cousin Dif said. "Is this everyone we're waiting for?"

"Should be," I said.

"Excellent," Dif replied.

Then, using my mother's gun, he shot Grandpa Smedry in the head.

Chapter

19

I don't
    I just I Can't
It
he
...

Okay. Yes. He shot Grandpa. Square in the face with a real gun. My grandfather collapsed backward without a sound.

I assume you think there is some trick here. I wish I could tell you something to make you happy.

Instead, let me make it clear: That bullet was real. After all his tricks and close calls, my grandfather—Leavenworth Smedry—finally found an end he could not escape.

Draulin was the first to react. She leaped for Dif, but a hail of glowing shots from right outside the room burst around him, and at least a dozen struck her. I recognized them as blasts from the coma guns used in the siege of Tuki Tuki.

That is to say, a piece of my mind recognized them. The rest of me just stood there stupidly, reeling from the sudden betrayal.

My father was far more alert. He ripped off his Translator's Lenses and raised the others.

Dif casually shot the spectacles out of Father's hand, causing the Concussor's Lens to explode, spraying my father's skin with shards of broken glass.

"Such brutal weapons, ordinary handguns," Dif said, striding forward, pistol in hand. His voice had changed. It was more calm, more straightforward, more quiet. "But one uses the tools offered."

He stopped beside me and placed the gun to my head. I found myself trembling, revealed as a coward once and for all. Draulin had tried to stop him; my father had tried to stop him. All I could do was stare.

Grandpa . . .

The barrel of the gun felt warm against my forehead.

"Stand down, Attica," Dif said. "Unless you want to be childless as well as fatherless."

"You *monster,*" my father said. He held his bloodied hand before him, but with the other hand had been reaching into his pocket—undoubtedly for another Lens. He stopped as Dif manually cocked the gun's hammer.

Librarian soldiers flooded across the walkway outside and into the room. These weren't the 'bow tie and spectacles' type I'd seen everywhere else. These were futuristic soldiers with helmets and black special forces gear, like you'd see in a movie.

"You're one of them," I whispered at Dif.

"I've learned a few things over the years fighting the Smedry clan," Dif said, stepping away from me as several soldiers grabbed my father by the arms and frisked him, taking his Lenses. "One is the power of a great infiltration. You people are always wriggling in among my agents and teams. I finally realized, why not return the favor?" He looked to me and smiled.

And in his eyes I saw a vastness. Knowledge, danger, and *depth* beyond anything that had been there before.

"No," I whispered. "You're not *a* Librarian. You're *the* Librarian."

Biblioden the Scrivener had been among us the entire time.

One of the soldiers walked up to him and saluted. "Area secure, my lord." He proffered a bag full of Lenses taken from my father.

"So you are him, I assume," Attica said with a sneer. "Or you *claim* to be him, and these others believe you."

"I fought your great-great-whatever-grandfather," Biblioden said, tucking away the pouch of Lenses. "He was almost as much a pain as you are. I knew you were in here somewhere, Attica. But where? And how? I was going to let my people find you, as I was too busy with my work at the Worldspire. But then this chance fell right in my lap! I couldn't resist."

He looked to my father. "I find it amazing that you have grown *worse* while I was away, you Smedrys. Like breeding rats."

"Your pretend Talent," I said, realizing it. "You chose it specifically because you knew nobody would be able to prove you didn't have one. And on the bridge, after we met the dinosaurs, the Dark Oculator fled not because

she recognized me—but because she recognized *you.*
I'd told her I worked for you, and she hadn't believed
me, so when you appeared she was terrified that she had
offended you."

Dif smiled.

"You broke my Truthfinder's Lens," I whispered. "But
how . . . how did you convince us . . . ?"

"I only had to convince your grandfather," Dif said.
"Years ago, you see. Kill a Smedry boy and his parents
living in the Hushlands, years later convince old Leavenworth I was the child, who had survived in the wilds of
the Hushlands on my own! It was mostly a way to get me
close to the Worldspire. Who would turn away a known
Smedry? And now . . . well, who could have guessed the
fruit my work would bear!"

He strolled to my father's desk and held out his palm,
and one of the soldiers scrambled to pick up the notebooks and hand them to him.

"Thank you," Dif said, "for gathering the Sands of
Rashid for me. The codes of the Incarna, such a frustrat-
ing puzzle. I . . . appreciate the work you have done here,
little rats. Very, *very* helpful."

Biblioden raised Father's first notebook and riffled
through it at high speed. A quick zip. "Ah. I see."

He offered to join us, I thought, remembering Grandpa

explaining that Dif had contacted him. *He kept trying to separate me from my mother. He's been playing us this entire mission.*

Dif zipped through a second book just as rapidly, then moved on to the next one. "Yes . . ."

He can't possibly be reading them so quickly, can he?

Zip. Another book done.

I needed to do something. They hadn't searched me, though several soldiers stood with guns trained on me. What did I have? My Shaper's Lens? Could I use that? I often found that the odd, information-based Lenses my grandfather gave me were surprisingly useful in times of tension.

Grandpa . . .

Don't think about that, I told myself forcefully. *He might still be alive.* People who got shot in the head survived sometimes, didn't they?

Squeezing my eyes shut as Biblioden continued his super-speed-read of my father's notes, I reached into my pocket and pulled out the Shaper's Lens. Shattering Glass! It was almost too hot to touch!

I carefully brought it up, then engaged it, looking through it at Biblioden the Scrivener, to see his deepest desires.

I saw this:

Darkness.

A deep, compelling darkness. Like an ocean at midnight. Or the vast emptiness of space, if all the stars had gone out. There was something alien, empty, and terrible about it that I cannot describe, and won't try.

I gasped and dropped the Lens.

"Yes," Biblioden said, setting aside the final notebook, "I was *hoping* you'd try that." He smiled.

That smile seemed to be lacking even the faintest *shred* of humanity. I stumbled back but ran into a soldier, who pressed his weapon between my shoulder blades.

"Thank you," Biblioden said, "for explaining that the Talents were broken." He nodded to the soldier behind me, and that man dug in my pocket. He took out the Courier's Lenses and flung them aside, then pulled out the mobile phone and tossed it to Biblioden.

The Scrivener dialed. "Hello, Cousin Kaz? It's Dif here!"

His voice had changed back to how it was before, all perky and energetic. I felt sick. I had taken him for a Smedry who was trying too hard, but now I saw what was really going on. This was how Biblioden viewed us, and his exaggerated caricature was his way of trying to imitate us.

I could barely hear Kaz's voice on the other end of the line. "Dif?" he asked. "What's going on? I have Himalaya's team."

"We're done in here!" Biblioden exclaimed. "It was *awesome.* Alcatraz used a lightbulb and two pieces of yak hair to solve the puzzle!"

"Sounds like him," Kaz said. "You have my brother?"

"Sure do, and a whole pile of Forgotten Language texts. Would you be willing to wait for us before taking off?"

"It's going to be hard...."

"But that's the Smedry way!" Biblioden exclaimed.

"All right. We'll do it. I—" An explosion sounded over the line. "Shattering Glass! *Penguinator* just took a hit! Dif, get here soon."

"Kaz?" Biblioden asked. "You okay?"

"Blasted thing can't take off now," Kaz's voice said over the line. "We're taking refuge in the archive room again! Bring Pop here quick. We'll need another plan."

"Sure. I can do that," Biblioden said, then smiled, hanging up. "Guess I needn't have bothered. The rocket crews did their job." He tossed the phone to one of his soldiers, who in turn lobbed it out the door and over the edge of the walkway. It plummeted down toward the overworked fans below.

I didn't even hear it crunch.

"Now, let's be off," Biblioden the Scrivener said. "There is much to do yet today."

"What are you planning, you tyrant?" my father demanded, struggling against his bonds.

"No need for language like that!" Biblioden said. "I'm going to *help* you, Attica. I'm going to put your research into motion! This is going to be very, *very* interesting."

Father's struggles were pointless; the soldiers marched him from the room. Two of them gathered up my mother, and two others took Draulin under the arms and dragged her away. They left Grandpa's corpse just lying there.

Draulin.

The cure!

I *had* it still, in my other pocket. But how in the world could I administer it to her without them seeing? My mind raced as they forced me, at gunpoint, to start following the others along the walkway. There was no getting to Draulin. There were too many guards between me and her.

But maybe . . .

That's reckless.

It was the only plan I had. It occurred to me, right then and there, that there was a reason behind the Smedry way. Not recklessness for the sake of being reckless, as Biblioden behaved. We acted like we did because we had no other options.

We were the ones willing to take the risk.

Wind whipping at my robe, I pulled out the bottle of

antidote and moved to run back toward the room with Grandfather's body. I was counting on the guards not wanting to kill me, and I was right, as one slammed the butt of his rifle into my side instead of shooting me.

I gasped in pain and fell to my knees, dropping the bottle of antidote. It bounced once, then rolled off the edge of the walkway.

"No!" I cried, reaching toward it as it fell.

Biblioden walked over as one of the soldiers pulled me to my feet. "Thinking of using that on old Grandpa Smedry? It doesn't cure *death*, child." He smiled at me.

I tried to punch him, but one of the guards took me by the arm before I could. Biblioden nodded, and another guard pulled my robe off and tossed it into the fans beneath. That left me in my tuxedo.

"Face this like a Smedry," Biblioden said, patting me on the shoulder. "It is a fitting way to end."

"What . . ." I gasped in a breath, holding my side where I'd been struck. "What are you going to do with us?"

"Surely you've figured that out," Biblioden said, strolling across the walkway. The soldiers marched me beside him, my father finally sagging in his bonds just ahead. "All of that power. I *wondered* what glories your father would discover, but even without reading the notebooks, I knew that there was something special about your line.

Something I wanted." He looked to me. "Have you ever watched a bloodforged Lens being made?"

I felt cold. *Oh no . . .*

"It's not as bad as it sounds," Biblioden said as we walked. "But from what I read in your father's research, this will be an *excellent* way to approach the Incarnate Wheel and beseech it for blessings. And beyond that . . . yes, I do think it will be quite possible to draw the energy source out from inside you and put it to my own use. Your father's research on the Worldspire tells me that I can transform people from a great distance. What if I made every person in the Free Kingdoms into a power source, like the Smedrys? What would *happen* to their society?"

He looked at me and smiled a terrible smile. "Why . . . there would be no more need for a war. Since the Free Kingdoms would go the way of Incarna. They'd simply. Stop. Existing."

That was the meaning of the darkness. An end to everything Biblioden saw as strange, bizarre, or uncontrollable. I shouted, thrashing, trying to escape as the soldiers hauled me back down the corridor.

We emerged into the central cavern. In the near distance, bathed in light from the open ceiling above, I saw the altar atop its stone peak.

Chapter

· 20 ·

So there it is; that's how I finally ended up tied to an altar made from outdated encyclopedias. Yes, I exaggerated a bit about the magma, fire, and sharks, but this part actually happened. I *was* about to get sacrificed to the dark powers by a cult of evil Librarians.

And that's how my grandfather got shot.

I lay there, strapped in place, as Biblioden and several Librarians from the Order of the Shattered Lens prepared the ceremony. And I couldn't help thinking about my parents.

What had gone wrong? Had there been one single event? A moment that drove a wedge between my father and mother? Both, deep down, wanted to be with one another. I'd *seen* it. Yet neither acted that way.

I wondered what the Shaper's Lens would show if it were turned on me. What did *I* want? More than anything?

I turned my head, the only part of my body that I could move. The spire with the altar was big enough for a few dozen people at the top, but I was close enough to the edge to look down the fifty feet or so and spot the place where—surrounded by soldiers—Kaz and Himalaya made their last stand. *Penguinator* lay in wreckage nearby, a gaping hole in its side.

I looked back toward the open ceiling as Biblioden strolled over to me.

I smiled at him.

"I did not expect you to smile," he noted, hands clasped behind his back. "Usually when people are approaching sacrifice, they are not happy about it."

"I'm going to beat you," I whispered.

"Smedry bravado," Biblioden said.

"I've been in worse situations than this," I said. "I always make it through unscathed. It will work out. You'll see."

"In those other situations, you weren't facing *me*," Biblioden said, then leaned down. "Do you realize what your family is, child? You are the *symbol* of everything loathsome in the world. Pretending to be one of you was the most difficult thing I've ever done. Worse than killing my brother. Worse than sinking a continent full of loyal followers because of the corruption that had spread among them. Worse than *anything*."

He grabbed me by the chin, forcing me to look into his eyes as he leaned down. "I am going to *relish* the chance to remove everything special, interesting, or distinctive about you people. When I'm done you'll be dead, and the rest of your family will be *normal*. Fitting, isn't it?"

He let go of me and stood up, looking toward my father, who was being held by two Librarian soldiers at the edge of the altar's platform.

"This ceremony," Biblioden proclaimed, "is more powerful if performed on a *willing* victim. So I'm going to give you two a chance. Once I'm done, on my word of honor, I will set one of you free. I'd rather you live and know what was done to you anyway."

What was that scent in the air?

"So which will it be?" Biblioden asked. "Which of you lives, and which dies? I'll let the two of you choose."

"Sir," said one of the soldiers. "Do you smell that? Smells like . . . cinnamon."

Biblioden paused.

Down below, the door to *Penguinator* shook with a resounding *bang*. Then it exploded open.

A small figure with silver hair stood in the doorway. A thirteen-year-old girl clutching a long crystalline sword.

She looked very, very angry.

"You dropped the antidote into the ventilation system on purpose," Biblioden said with a groan. "I should have seen that. Well, what does it matter? She's only one person."

"You," I said, "have never dealt with Bastille in a bad mood."

The soldiers started firing. I almost felt sorry for them.

Biblioden watched for a moment, but unfortunately the angle wasn't right for me to see more of what was happening below. His eyes widened, and then he stepped back.

"All right," he announced, looking to the others. "Time to speed this up. Roger, knock down the steps leading here. Everyone else, start firing in that direction. Smedrys, make your decision *now*."

"Well," I said, grinning and trying to stall. "I just need a moment to think. . . ."

Biblioden pulled out my mother's handgun and pressed it to my temple. "Choose!"

I stammered, trying to delay. But as I did, I started to

worry. Bastille had a lot of distance to cover. Even if she did get here, how was she going to fight her way up to us? She was incredible, but she wasn't omnipotent.

"I'll count to three," Biblioden said. "One."

Stall. I had to stall! "No, listen, I know where you can find much more power—"

"Two."

There *had* to be a way out of this. I felt a panic. A sudden, *overwhelming* panic. "Don't do this. I know something you don't. I have secrets!"

"Three."

"Take me!" my father cried out. Right as I said something.

"Take him."

Deep down, in that moment of crisis, I didn't want to die. I can tell myself it was because I thought it would waste more of their time to take me off the altar and put him there instead.

But in the end, I just didn't want to die.

Chapter

• 21 •

They found me huddled up in a ball on the platform, a bloodied altar of books behind me.

I'll avoid describing what they did to my father. But his corpse was on that altar.

"Alcatraz?" Bastille's voice.

I stared sightlessly, trying to banish from my mind what I'd just seen.

"Oh, Glass, no!" Kaz's voice. "Attica . . ."

A shape moved past me toward the altar. I wasn't looking.

I'd seen far too much already.

"Kaz, we have to *go*." Draulin? Of course. They'd left her at the base of the pillar, unconscious, but she'd have woken up too. The antidote . . .

"Alcatraz." Bastille sounded exhausted. "Who was up here with you? A ship flew down and carried them off. Why did they leave you? Can you hear me?"

No.

I didn't want to hear.

"Pick him up, Bastille," Draulin said, her voice hard. "With Leavenworth and Attica dead, Alcatraz is now the last member of the direct Smedry line. We must get him to safety."

"They're scattering quickly," Kaz said, his voice tense with grief. "I think the Librarian leaders must not have turned off the detonation that Pop set up. Why would they abandon so much? The Highbrary itself? And my brother . . . What is going *on* here?"

Too many people saw strange things here, I wanted to whisper. *So Biblioden is going to sacrifice them.*

I couldn't say it. Not with the sound of my father's screams in my ears. I squeezed my eyes shut.

And let them carry me away.

Author's Afterword

Yes, that's it.

I tried to prepare you. I told you this was the ending, and that you weren't going to like it.

The self-destruct device went off about an hour after we escaped. The Highbrary was destroyed, though it was passed off as an earthquake, as most of the destruction was underground. It did cause chaos in Washington, DC, which was already suffering from the battle that had taken place in the skies.

But the Librarians rebuilt it. Covered it up with some renovation project or another. They carefully went about interviewing people and finding out if they'd seen my speech. Then the Librarians wiped their memories of the event. It took forever, but they managed it.

Everything went back to normal.

I failed.

I can sense that you want more. I can sense that you're expecting this story to continue. It won't; I'm done. I'm no hero, and the truth is now out. That's why I wrote these books.

In that moment when I could have sacrificed myself, I told them to take my father instead. My father, the man who could have stopped Biblioden. The man who understood more than anyone else about Lenses, the Incarna, and the nature of our enemies.

I let him die because I was too much of a coward to take his place.

With this, I end my autobiography. I won't thank you for reading it. This was something you *needed* to read. Just like it was something I *needed* to say.

It is finally over.

I'm sorry.

THE END

ABOUT THE AUTHOR

Brandon Sanderson is the fake author of these books, the name Alcatraz publishes them under to keep the Librarians from realizing that the books are real. Alcatraz has it on good authority that while there was once an actual Brandon Sanderson, he was executed for taking too much time to write the fifth book of a series—and then doing something horrible at the ending. These days, the title "Brandon Sanderson" is wielded by a group of shadowy book-writing ninjas, with the goal of owning all of the world's mac and cheese.

ABOUT THE ILLUSTRATOR

In addition to her work as an illustrator, Hayley Lazo has recently committed herself to such philanthropic movements as No Shark Left Behind and the Kitten Rehabilitation Initiative. Surprisingly, she hasn't lost any fingers yet, and insists that she could still manage to draw even if one or two were to go missing. Her art can be found at art-zealot.deviantart.com.

ACKNOWLEDGMENTS

This one was a long time coming! I offer many apologies for that, along with many, many thanks to the people who helped this come to pass.

First off, thank you to those at Tor Books, Tor Teen, and Starscape Books who picked up this series and helped it rise from the ashes to come back to life. Susan Chang is the editor. She wanted this series badly from the start, and has long been a champion of Alcatraz and his insanity. Her team at Starscape/Tor included Megan Kiddoo, Karl Gold, Victoria Wallis, Deanna Hoak, and Rafal Gibek. Also, thanks to Kathleen Doherty for believing in me and even my most insane projects.

You may have noticed the awesome artwork in this edition. I'm very pleased with how this turned out. Hayley Lazo did the interior art, and she is just magnificent. Also, a special thanks to Scott Brundage, who did the cover. For the first time I feel I have a cover illustrator who really gets the Alcatraz books. His covers are brilliant, and rank among my favorite covers on any of my books ever.

My team at Dragonsteel includes Isaac Stewart who did the gorgeous map for these editions—and who was also the art director for the project. He put in a lot of extra effort on these books.

The inaugural Peter Ahlstrom did his normal brilliant editing job. It swamped him, getting all five books ready for publication, but he soldiered on like a Smedry. The rest of my team includes Kara Stewart, Karen Ahlstrom, Adam Horne, and Emily Sanderson.

Thanks to my agents, Eddie Schneider and Joshua Bilmes, as always.

Beta readers included Peter Ahlstrom, Aaron Rothman, Darci Cole, Randy MacKay, Frances Moritz, Cassandra Moritz, Gideon Roberts, Anda Jones, Caleb Jones, Hylke Damien, Kristina Kugler, Brenna Kugler, Jonas Kugler, Christine Wilkinson, Lindy Wilkinson, Emily Wilkinson, Haley Wilkinson, Audrey Horne, Ariana Horne, Jaclyn Weist, Jakob Weist, Ashley Weist, Andy Weist, Steve Weist, Briana Farr, Libby Glancy, Margaret Glancy, Jaxon Kremser, Josh Walker, Mi'chelle Walker, Mike Shaffer, Trevor Florence, Calvin Florence, Tomas Cundick, Annabel Cantor, Kacee Garner, Isaac Garner, Karen Ahlstrom, and Isaac Stewart.

Gamma readers included many of the above, plus Anna Hornbostel, Gary Singer, Louis Hill, Megan Kanne, Rebecca Arneson, Alice Arneson, Trae Cooper, Ross Newberry, Mark Lindberg, Jana S. Brown, Sarah "Saphy" Hansen, Kellyn Neumann, and Bonny Skarstedt.

Starscape Reading and Activity Guide to the Alcatraz vs. the Evil Librarians Series
By Brandon Sanderson

Ages 8–12; Grades 3–7

About This Guide

The questions and activities that follow are intended to enhance your reading of Brandon Sanderson's Alcatraz novels. The guide has been developed in alignment with the Common Core State Standards, however please feel free to adapt this content to suit the needs and interests of your students or reading group participants.

About the Alcatraz Series

Brandon Sanderson turns readers' understanding of literary genres upside down and backwards in this lively adventure series. In the world of thirteen-year-old Alcatraz Smedry, "Librarians," with their compulsions to organize and control information, are a source of evil, and "Talents" can include breaking things, arriving late, and getting lost. Add an unlikely teenage knight named Bastille, flying glass dragons, wild battles, references to philosophers and authors from Heraclitus to Terry Pratchett, and plenty of hilarious wordplay, and you have a series to please book lovers of all ages. And one that will have readers reflecting deeply about the nature of knowledge, truth, family, and trust, all while laughing out loud.

READING LITERATURE

Genre Study: Fantasy

In the introduction to the first book in the series, *Alcatraz vs. the Evil Librarians,* the narrator, Alcatraz Smedry, claims that his story is true, even though it will be shelved as "fantasy" in the world to which his readers (you) belong.

Fantasy is a literary genre that often includes:
- Characters who are magical, inspired by mythology, or who have special powers
- Settings that include unexplored parts of the known world, or new and different worlds
- Plot elements (actions) that cannot be explained in terms of historical or scientific information from our known world

While reading the books in this series, note when the author uses some of these elements of fantasy to tell his story. Students can track their observations in reading journals if desired, noting which elements of the fantasy genre are most often used by the author.

Older readers (grades 6 and 7) may also consider the way the author incorporates elements of the following genres into his novels, as well as how these genres relate to the fantasy components of the series:

Science fiction, which deals with imaginative concepts such as futuristic settings and technologies, space and time travel, and parallel universes. Science fiction stories frequently explore the effects of specific scientific or technological discoveries on governments and societies.

Steampunk, a subgenre of science fiction, which is often set in an alternative history or fantasy and features the use of steam as a primary power source. Steampunk features technologies which seem simultaneously futuristic and old-fashioned, or beings which are combinations of mechanical and biological elements.

After reading one or more of the Alcatraz books, invite students to reread the "Author's Foreword" to *Alcatraz vs. the Evil Librarians* and discuss why they think the author chose to begin the series by explaining where the books will be shelved in a library.

Technical Study: Structure and Literary Devices

The Alcatraz series can be viewed as the author's exploration of the idea, concept, and value of books themselves as both a way information is shared, and the way it is contained. One way Brandon Sanderson accomplishes this is to question the very structure of the novel. Invite students to look for the following elements in the stories and share their reactions to these literary devices and structures.

- Point of View. In this series, the point of view through which the reader sees the story is in the first-person voice of Alcatraz Smedry. He also claims that he is using the name Brandon Sanderson as a pseudonym, thus this is an autobiography or memoir. Is Alcatraz Smedry a *reliable* narrator, giving readers an unbiased report of the events of the story, or is Al an *unreliable* narrator, making false claims or telling the story in such a way as to leave doubts in the reader's mind? In what ways is Alcatraz reliable and/or unreliable? How might the series be different if Bastille or another character were telling the story? (Hint: For further examples of unreliable narrators in children's and teen fiction, read Jon Scieszka's *The True Story of the Three Little Pigs*, E. Nesbit's *The Story of the Treasure Seekers*, Justine Larbalestier's *Liar*, or Harper Lee's *To Kill a Mockingbird*.)
- Asides. At times, the narrator directly addresses the reader, suggesting how s/he should interpret a comment or how to best enjoy the novel (e.g. reading aloud or acting out scenes). Does this change the reader's sense of his or her relationship with the book? If so, how does this relationship feel different?

- <u>Chapter Breaks</u>. Discuss the unusual ways the author begins, ends, numbers, and sequences chapters. Is this pleasant or unpleasant? Have readers read any other works of fiction (or nonfiction) that explore chapters in this way?
- <u>Wordplay in World-Building</u>. To explain *Free Kingdoms* ideas, technologies, and objects in terms of the *Hushlander* (readers') world, the author uses similes, metaphors, and analogies. To reflect protagonist Alcatraz's own confusion and frustration, Brandon Sanderson employs invented words, puns, and even text written backwards or in other unusual ways. Find examples of these uses of wordplay in the text. How does the use of these literary devices enrich the text?

Character Study: Families and Friends

Having been raised in foster homes convinced that both of his parents were horrible people, Alcatraz Smedry is often uncertain as to what it means to like, love, and trust other people. Since he is the narrator of the series, Alcatraz's uncertainty affects readers' perceptions of the characters he describes. In a reading journal or in class discussion, have students analyze the physical traits, lineage (parents, relationships), motivations, and concerns of major characters in the novel. How is each character related to Alcatraz? What is especially important about the idea of family relationships in this series? Does Alcatraz's view of certain characters change in the course of single books? Do recurring characters develop or change over the course of more than one book in the series? If so, how and why do the characters evolve?

English Language Arts Common Core Reading Literature Standards
RL.3.3-6, 4.3-6, 5.3-6, 6.3-6, 7.3-6

THEMES AND MOTIFS: DISCUSSION TOPICS
for the ALCATRAZ SERIES

Sanderson's Alcatraz novels can be read on many levels, including as adventure stories, as musings on the nature of knowledge, and as fantasies incorporating elements of science fiction and steampunk. Here are some themes you may want to watch for and explore with your classmates or students.

- Talent. How does Sanderson use the word *talent* in traditional and nontraditional ways? Is talent important, valuable, even essential? What does Sanderson really mean by "talent"? How might students incorporate Sanderson's unique interpretation of the word talent into their own sense of self?
- Heroism. Throughout the novel, Alcatraz claims to be "bad," "a liar," "a coward," and "not a hero." What makes a "hero" in a novel, a movie, and in real life? Does it matter if a person acts heroically on purpose or by accident? What do you think is the most important reason Alcatraz denies his heroism?
- Knowledge, Learning, Thinking. Find instances in the stories when Alcatraz admits to acting before thinking ahead to consider all possible outcomes of his plans. In these instances, is he simply being careless or does he lack some important information since he was raised in the Hushlands? Compare and contrast the way people acquire knowledge in the Hushlands versus the Free Kingdoms.
- Opposites. Throughout the novels, the narrator refers to the ideas of the ancient Greek philosopher Heraclitus, whose doctrines included (1) universal flux (the idea that things are constantly changing) and (2) unity of opposites (the idea that opposites (objects, ideas) are necessary and balance each other). The philosopher also believed that "Much learning does not teach understanding," (*The Art and Thought of*

Heraclitus, ed. Charles H. Kahn, Cambridge University Press, 1981). How might the series be read as an exploration of Heraclitus's doctrines?

English Language Arts Common Core Speaking and Listening Standards
SL.3.1, 4.1, 5.1, 6.1, 7.1
SL.3.3, 4.3, 5.3, 6.3, 7.3

RESEARCH AND WRITING PROJECTS

Keep a Reading Journal.

Use the journal to record:

- Favorite quotations, funny lines, exciting scenes (note page numbers).
- Situations in which the main character is in crisis or danger, and notes on what advice readers might offer.
- New vocabulary words and/or a list of invented words.
- Sketches inspired by the novels.
- Questions readers would like to ask the author or characters from the novels.

Explore Glass.

From Oculators' Lenses to unbreakable glass buildings, glass is a core substance throughout the series. Go to the library or online to learn more about glass. Create a PowerPoint or other multimedia presentation discussing the physical properties, history, practical, and creative uses of glass. Or create a presentation explaining how glass works in the Free Kingdoms. Include visual elements, such as photographs or drawings, in your presentation.

Silimatic Technology.

This part scientific, part magical technology powers much of the Free Kingdoms. Using details from the novels, create an outline or short pamphlet explaining the rules and functions of silimatic technology as you understand it. If desired, dress as you imagine a Free Kingdoms scientist might choose to dress and present your findings to classmates.

Choose a Talent.

Many of the characters in the Alcatraz series have talents that seem more like problems. Think of a personality or quality you consider a fault in your own life, such as messy penmanship, bad spelling, or the inability to catch a baseball. Imagine how that talent might prove useful in the world of Alcatraz. Write a 3–5 page scene in which you encounter Alcatraz and help him using your "talent."

English Language Arts Common Core Writing Standards
W.3.1-3, 4.1-3, 5.1-3, 6.1-3, 7.1-3
W3.7-8, 4.7-9, 5.7-9, 6.7-9, 7.7-9

DISCUSSION STARTERS AND WRITING PROMPTS FOR INDIVIDUAL TITLES

THE DARK TALENT

To stop his father from carrying out a dastardly plan to unleash Talents across the Hushlands, Alcatraz must infiltrate his dad's hiding place within the Evil Librarian's great Highbrary—cunningly disguised as the Library of Congress. But can he trust his accomplices, including his terrifying mother Shasta and annoying cousin Dif? And, with his own Talent dangerously disabled, will he be able to find his father in time to save anyone—even himself?

QUOTES

Discuss the following quotations in terms of what they mean in terms of the novel; in terms of your thoughts about books and libraries; and in terms of their relevance to the real lives of readers.

The [tales] we tell ourselves these days always seem to need a happy ending. . . . Is it because the Librarians are protecting us from stories with sad endings? Or is it something about who we are, who we have become as a society, that makes us need to see the good guys win?
(Chapter Mary)

"Have you been with that fool of a grandfather of yours so long you've lost the ability to see the world as it has *to be?"*
(Chapter 16)

"Librarians," my mother said, "share more with Smedrys than either would like to admit."
(Chapter 17)

Father said. "Son, you have to understand. Your mother is a Librarian. *In her heart, she's terrified of change—not to mention frightened of the idea of common people being outside her control."*
(Chapter 18)

WRITING EXERCISES

Reading Journal Entry: Cowardice

Beginning with the Foreword, through chapters Shu Wei and 19, to the final pages of the Afterword, Alcatraz repeatedly calls himself a coward. Do you think Alcatraz is a coward in any or all of these instances? Write a journal entry explaining how you think Alcatraz would define the term coward, whether you use this term in the same way in your own life, and how you feel toward Alcatraz at moments in the story when he sees himself as a coward.

Reading Journal Entry: Has Alcatraz Failed?

Write a journal entry in which you agree or disagree with Alcatraz's final page apologia. Has he failed and, if so, whom has he failed? Use quotes from the Evil Librarians series and/or from other novels or poems you have read to support your position.

Explanatory Text: Smedrys

Throughout the novel, Alcatraz, Kaz, Dif, and other characters refer to certain actions or ideas as typical of members of the Smedry line. In the character of Grandpa, Attica, Shasta, or Dif, write an essay explaining what it means to be a Smedry. Or, in the character of Alcatraz, write a letter to Bastille describing how you feel about belonging to the Smedry family.

Explanatory Text: Aesop's Fables

Brandon Sanderson makes several references to fables, particularly Aesop's Fables, in *The Dark Talent*. With friends or classmates, go to the library or online to find a definition of "fable" and some facts about Aesop and his literary legacy. Read several of Aesop's fables and select one that you feel could be applied to a scene in the novel. Write a short essay explaining why you believe Sanderson wanted to incorporate the idea of fables into this novel, and how and where you would reference your selected fable within the book.

Literary Analysis: Authorship

The Evil Librarians series is narrated by the character Alcatraz Smedry, who claims to be using the pseudonym of "Hushlands" author Brandon Sanderson. With friends or classmates, discuss how this double-layered claim of authorship affects the reading of the book and/or the reader's relationship with the narrator. Then, individually, write a short essay interpreting the following quote by Pulitzer Prize–winning author Junot Diaz in terms of the Evil Librarians novels you have read:

We all dream that there's an authoritative voice out there that will explain things, including ourselves. If it wasn't for our longing for these things, I doubt the novel or the short story would exist in its current form.

English Language Arts Common Core Standards
RL.3.1-4, 4.1-4, 5.1-4, 6.1-4, 7.1-4
SL.3.3-4, 4.3-4, 5.3-4, 6.3-4, 7.3-4
W.3.1-3, 4.1-3, 5.1-3, 6.1-3, 7.1-3; W3.7-8, 4.7-9, 5.7-9, 6.7-9, 7.7-9

Read all the books in the Alcatraz vs. the Evil Librarians series!

Alcatraz vs. the Evil Librarians

The Scrivener's Bones

The Knights of Crystallia

The Shattered Lens

The Dark Talent

DO NOT OPEN
UNTIL YOU FINISH READING THE BOOK